PURITY

AIRSHIP 27 PRODUCTIONS

TM

Published by Airship 27 Productions
www.airship27.com
www.airship27hangar.com

Interior illustrations © 2020 Rob Davis
Cover illustration © 2020 Michael Youngblood

Editor: Ron Fortier
Associate Editor: Fred Adams Jr.
Marketing and Promotions Manager: Michael Vance
Production and design by Rob Davis

ISBN: 978-1-946183-94-1

Printed in the United States of America

10 9 8 7 6 5 4 3 2 1

MARK JUSTICE'S
The Dead SHERIFF
PURITY

by

MICHAEL HOUSEL

PROLOGUE

Princeton, New Jersey 1829

The wind whipped and snapped, ripping shingles and rapping panes. Even at a tender two years of age, Palmer Perdifious detected the danger and as such, desired protection, perhaps more so, escape. If only his parents would come and take him away from the raucous rage.

When the storm commenced, he had heard them debating in the dining room about the scarcity of shipping-company funds. They speculated as to when their posh, Princeton abode would slip from their prestigious grasp. What then would they do? What would the neighbors say? Would they offer compassion, pity or ridicule? Most likely ridicule. Perhaps this was why his parents ignored him. Keeping a roof over their heads was a far greater concern than the babe who slept under one.

A branch smacked the glass, its uneven tendrils sliding like sharp nails. He bounced into a sitting position and grabbed the crib's wooden bars. No doubt those dark, spindly strands wished to clutch him, harm him. Oh, what had he done to spur such fury?

Just as the branch broke the glass, he cried for mercy, its tendrils fanning within the tussling blast.

The storm curled about his chamber, knocking loose the duckling mobile from above his crib and a dimmed lamp from off his bureau. The latter shattered, its small flame proving impervious to the torrential sweep, skidding across the wooden floor, onto his little, arabesque rug, prancing ever higher and wider, as if imbued by a supernatural force.

Heat cooked his cheeks. Smoke stung his throat.

Perhaps if he ignored the heat and noise, he could withstand the storm's contradictory calamity. Perhaps if he suckled the sprawling flames, embraced the hammering gale, he would draw their strength. Perhaps if he prayed to these teeming elements, surrendered himself to their hateful onslaught, they would grant him release, maybe even strike a deal with him so that he might live.

He saw within each ascending flicker, amorphous bodies flapping, red like robins with long, wide wings, horned crowns and spidery fingers. They took the place of his dangling ducks, going round and round with eyes black, piercing and oh-so-omniscient.

He was too young to understand the meaning of a Faustian pact, and yet his demons offered it per their cobbled words and disjointed phrases until a cohesive temptation was born: "You will see clearer than others see, see all the good and bad that is to be and is to come, but if you wish to survive—to rule, Palmer Perdifious—you must embrace your powers unconditionally. It is only through you that we, the demons of your mind, shall usher your requests."

His cheeks blistered, the poisonous flow demanding his consent. He gave it gladly, for he wished not to die, but to fly, to soar, as did his mercurial monsters, moving ever faster, so bright, fluid and fierce above his head.

"Indeed, you will soar, little Palmer Perdifious, but in your own way, on your own terms. You will unfold the annals of your burgeoning mind, become impervious to sorrow and pain, a master of your own accursed accord, with ideas sprung from the seeds that no child should or could fathom, and yet here you are, with a mind—and soul—redefined."

He envisioned his father rushing through the door, grabbing him, but the vision was at best hazy and loose. It was then prophetically followed by footsteps, his mother telling his father that something was wrong, that they must move faster.

But by then, the fire had scarred young Perdifious and with this, the profane pact had been not only sealed but dispatched.

"You now belong to us, the sons of Hades, the sons of merciless might— the sons of you, wee Palmer Perdifious, whose mind expands beyond his years to comprehend all that ever was or will be."

His father burst through the door, swatting the bustling smoke, cutting through the flames. He reached into the crib, wrapped his son into the blanket, hunkered and dashed into the hall.

"My, God, Peter, is he all right?"

"I don't know, Pamela. Let's get him downstairs, and from there we'll see."

Into the candle-lit living room and among all that rich mahogany, they paused. His father tugged the blanket from his son's face. His mother gasped.

"His face," she exclaimed. "Oh, his face, Peter. Dear, oh, dear."

"He needs a doctor, Pamela. We've no time to waste."

The flames continued to spread, along with the Tartarean heat, scooting down the stairwell, empowered by jeering, antithetical deceit.

Into the coach they raced. Hooves and wheels spun, but even with his eyes shut, little Perdifious could see his home collapsing, years stretching before him: his parents losing their self-regard, hiding him from the masses, pretending he was never born, but even so, Palmer Perdifious held no resentment. His parents would only do what was necessary, what he, himself, would do if the same circumstances were dealt.

Besides, he had a better family now, with wings, horns and glib voices, which understood his every whim. Through his new clan, a new Hell would spawn. It was only a matter of how to nurture its fiery poison, but nurture it he would, no matter who or what dared stand it his way.

It was his unswerving, contemptuous right, his carved-in-stone fate.

CHAPTER ONE

Thirty-eight Years Later

The Master's mind probed a mist that blew from everywhere and nowhere: his monstrous thought pattern etched with the thirst for vengeance.

More than anything, the Master desired the stolen amulet. It had slipped through the fingers of one of his agents, a suave, ginger-haired pawn called Lebine, and now it hung around the neck of an unworthy Indian named Cheveyo, otherwise known as Sam.

With this amulet, the Indian manipulated a hulking corpse to strike fear into the hearts of evildoers and as a side benefit, collected their bounties after he captured—or more so—killed them. Now in league with a Bostonian reporter named O'Malley, Sam continued to travel, infuriating the Master by evading his disciples one by one.

With this plaguing realization, the Master focused his mad might on the task at hand, dipping into acidic pits and foul trenches (unexplored territory even by his vile standards), until a bright, green slime bubbled and fumed from the blackness.

"Find the Indian," the Master beseeched as the globular form splashed upon his mind's eye. "Stop the evil that stops evil. Return the amulet to me."

The spectral substance rumbled and rose, carrying with it a telepathic milieu.

Instinct filled the Master, and he knew that through this thing's blind eyes, it saw all that it needed to see. It wasted no time to lick the vibrational residue about it; making sense of the nonsensical, believing success was within reach, even though the odds said otherwise.

The Master's heart brimmed with assurance, for he knew this entity would set the stage by enlisting the essential characters for a new, beleaguered play—one in which he would at long last find what was never meant to be lost.

FROM THE JOURNAL OF RICHARD O'MALLEY:

We have experienced a prolific run, trekking in ways that I could never have imagined, growing weary and yet pressing on in spite of it, returning often to the same, sorrowful spots. Time and again, we evade the Master and whatever minions he dispatches, but it is often difficult to identify them until it is too late. By design, they could be anyone or anything.

Still, there is money to be had, and money ensures survival. As my readers know, my partner, Sam (alias Cheveyo, or should that go the other way around?) keeps this conviction close to his heart and proves its necessity with the criminals that he (albeit through indirect measure) confronts and kills. Some come with lofty bounties, which feed and clothe us in better ways than we dare require. (Yes, my life savings has paved a solid foundation for my venture, but why deplete it when other financial means are available.) Our supplemental income (for a lack of a better term) has, therefore, allowed me to procure a steady supply of pencils, journals, cigars and wardrobe embellishments: all of which I store in a chest at the rear of our wagon, which thus far has not become tainted by the stench of our solemnized bread and butter: the Dead Sheriff.

I still do not know how the corpse heals or why he does. I simply accept his obvious, manipulated need to instill recurring comeuppances. Nevertheless, the Dead Sheriff does display moments of autonomy, a twitch or stride that comes as if from nowhere, though I have dismissed these gestures as mere leaps of command from Sam's unwitting mind. I do believe Sam rationalizes these gestures in much the same way, even though he is not much inclined to philosophize. For whatever cause, the Sheriff's actions now enforce a legend that has become as grand as that of any masked crusader, only with a far rougher, less pretentious edge.

Tonight we deliver the Dead Sheriff to Chesterfield, where we suspect two bad men remain "concealed": Ronald Fink and Timothy Fuller. The former shot dead a deputy in Peach Water when he and Fuller were robbing a bank: the most recent in a long string of such, though this was the only that resulted in death. To accentuate their reign of terror, they did their dirty deeds unmasked and were quick to toss their names about wherever they roamed. Though they may have evaded capture, they sure as hell nurtured their notoriety. Sam obtained their posters from an outpost and alive or dead (though with the Sheriff on hand, the latter is inevitable), we will soon have another copious sum to sustain our quasi-luxurious lifestyle.

I do trust, therefore, that our next stop will prove fast and fruitful, though as with any venture, there is the chance that our luck may run out.

This notion touches home more than usual, for I cannot deny a peculiar sensation about the air. It even permeates the look of the sky. I have mentioned my detection to Sam, but he dismisses it. However, I still discern an underlying concern in his eyes. If he senses the same, overriding doom, then perhaps we have cause for concern. Luck is a vicarious thing, influenced by any number of variables.

There is no denying that we toy with supernatural forces, after all. Their ultimate consequences could put us out of commission. If that should occur, what then do we do? So much rides upon the Sheriff's success, and without that, there is no money to gain, no legend to maintain.

Odd that I now place so much stock in that hideous corpse. When my old friend, Thunderstorm Parker, had told me of the Sheriff, I presumed the myth a novelty: one worth investigating and promoting. I have since come to realize that the Sheriff wields extraordinary significance beyond a mere fable, but does Sam, or any man, have the right to propel the thing?

Sam has told me (albeit through his inadvertent trances) that there are many factions that define our world. The smaller gods distinguish those factions. Do we have the right to pit one side against the other, let alone determine which ones benefit us? Do we have the right to make the Dead Sheriff avenge in the name of good if he is a product of bad?

I know my father, that ol' Irish Catholic and staunch Bostonian constable, frowned upon evil. I assume he would have denounced Sam's bizarre arrangement and my allegiance to it. However, I also do suspect that if he had considered the matter in depth, in particular from a policeman's analytical vantage, he might have seen its profane practicality.

Despite the internal debate, one thing remains certain: The Master is on our tails. No matter what we do, we are tied to him. At this point, even if we were to return the amulet, we would be no better for it. I fear we have dug our own proverbial hole and therefore, our inevitable grave. When playing with fire, one will get burnt, and in that rests our dilemma, our carved-in-stone fate. Alas, it is what it is: irreversible and for better or worse, for good or bad, entrenched.

Sam waxed his hopes, but Chesterfield was not a promising spot when it came to trust. The down-on-their-luck frequented it, as well as all the unsavory and unkind. To worsen the distasteful pot, its citizenry kept its collective lips sealed. The "law" did little to discourage the habit. Hardened criminals appreciated the nettling habit.

Thus far, O'Malley had visited the barber shop with the pretense of getting a trim, if only to inquire about bad men on the run. (The backward town had no newspaper, and so there was no journalistic reference of crime or related clues.) As expected, none of the shop's scraggy loungers fessed up, even though their shifty eyes conveyed knowledge. As a result, the brunt of inquiry was left to Sam. If his instincts were correct, success was right within his grasp.

At the moment, he sipped whisky (watered down, but wasn't it always?) at the corner table of a saloon/brothel, the wanted posters tugged and flattened, his ears pricked for any tidbit they might attract. After all, the men he sought were right under his nose, so close he could practically smell them, but a prerequisite shove was still required to prompt their ultimate reveal.

Eyeing him was a fetching, olive-skinned woman in a snug, black dress, high-heeled boots and an oversized bow looped within her raven hair. An elderly, honey-haired madam had passed her several times in the keep-the-customers-happy interim, nudging her his way, but thus far, the exotic beauty had prolonged the cat-and-mouse game.

Only after Sam had cracked a smile (the result of a liquored hiccup) did she then make her move, swaying over in such a way that made it hard to say no. Alas, Sam realized this was not the time for fleshy indulgences. Besides, regardless of the lass's allure, she could not help but remind him of his mother and those dismal days in New Orleans. There was also that matter of those bloodsucking variants he had come to know. Ah, but who was he kidding? This siren was as common to the trade as one might pluck from these parts: a mere, tempting commodity, if one so chose her.

"Hello," she purred, her Italian accent bewitching. "My name is Nita. What's yours, stranger?"

Sam wondered if his monosyllable act might be more suitable in this instance, but then settled on something in-between. "Cheveyo."

"Cheveyo." She rolled her eyes, relishing its breathy sound. "Nice name."

"So is yours."

Her perfume was strong, ebbing and flowing, telling him that in her eyes, he constituted more than a monetary tryst.

"You want company, Cheveyo? I do cost more than the other girls, but for good reason." Her lips curled. "So, what do you say? You, um, want to poke Nita?"

He was about to say yes, but caught himself. "Not at the moment, ma'am."

She assumed he was joking and hiked her skirt, exposing a long, coppery leg. "What you mean, not at the moment?" She smiled, her eyes sparkling. "Come now. How can you say no to Nita?"

She made a valid point, but he held his ground. "I've business to tend to first. Maybe later." He cranked an unconvincing smile. "Later, all right?"

Her nostrils flared. "Maybe there won't be a later."

He looked away, swallowing his temptation all the harder. "Then my loss."

"Ah, to hell with you." She threw up her hands and clicked away. The madam rushed over. The two began to argue. The madam pointed to Sam with insistence, but the sultry harlot continued to shake her head and stomp her heels. Oh, well, thought Sam. At least dear Nita was a woman of principle.

Once the exchange subsided, a batch of older, droopy-capped gents decided it was as good a time as any to approach the Indian.

"You a bounty hunter?" asked the first.

Sam patted the overlapped posters. "Yes."

"Indians are good at trackin'," another said.

"Rumor has it."

"Apache?"

"Can't say. Maybe."

"Well, you oughta know," remarked a third, swirling his finger at Sam's long hair and red head band. "You dress in the middle, but that glint in your eye, it's Apache awright."

"Then I'm Apache." Sam slid his bottle toward them and signaled the bartender for glasses, but the first man had already begun guzzling.

"Now that ain't polite," the second scolded.

"That's right," snapped the third. "You stingy bastard."

The first gent, the most weathered of the three, plopped into the chair across from Sam, a trickle of booze dripping from his fuzzy chin. "You'll catch these here fellers, won't you?"

Sam finished his glass and slammed it down. "Well, I'm not sitting here just to admire the artwork on these here posters. Studying the details and then scoping the terrain is my job."

"Makes sense," the coot confessed. "I'll say, it's bad enough that these criminals go round takin' other people's earnings, but then one of 'em goes and kills a man—a lawman, no less—in cold blood. I can only imagine what Frank Jackson's family is thinkin'. A wife, two sons and a daughter, don't you know? He always did right by 'em and by us, even if he did get a bit big for his britches, taking that stuffy deputy post in Peach Water. That's where he got himself killed, you know."

"Learned it from the documented details, my friend. Might you have a notion where these men are hiding? You see, I've a strong hunch they're somewhere in Chesterfield."

The old-timer shrugged. "Uh, dunno. Men come and go here. Me and my friends stay clear of those sorts, anyhow. Why look for trouble?"

Sam stood with slow, steely intent. "They haven't by chance paid you to keep quiet, have they?"

The old-timer frowned, leaving his friends to nudge each other and shuffle off. "Ah, no, sir."

Sam squinted with doubt. "They sure got a hefty load from the Peach Water Bank. I bet they'd spread some of that around, secure themselves a few lookouts."

"Wouldn't know." The old-timer swallowed hard. "Now, if you'd excuse me, sir."

Sam noticed the man's friends had headed upstairs. He gave the bartender a glance. In response, the portly man fought a quiver.

The old-timer got up and waddled away. He glanced up at his friends, hesitated a moment, but then exited the establishment. Sam then saw his friends knocking at one of the doors.

Belligerent groaning came from inside, capped by a woman's shrill giggle. Another knock followed, more profanity, more giggling, tipped by nervous whispering. Shortly thereafter, the uncouth gents descended and exited the premises, while avoiding Sam's glance.

Without further ado, the bartender ducked behind the bar. Patrons either scooted to the sidelines or squirmed under their tables. Sam cupped his gun and glided backward.

"Where da hell is he?" an emerging cowboy bellowed, popping from the room where the old men had knocked. His pimples were as visible as was his unkempt hair. Sam recognized his face from the poster—Fink. "So, where is this goddamn Injun?"

Behind Fink , another cowboy emerged, his long locks bobbing—Fuller. "Yeah, where are you, Injun? You lookin for us to make a few dollars?"

Sam pressed himself against the wall.

"Hey, there he is," Fink proclaimed as he skipped into a slow descent. "Tryin' to hide, eh?"

"Is that it, Injun—you gone yellow on us?" Fuller snickered, his eyes catching Sam. "Well, I'll be, I do believe you have."

No sooner had the two cocked their guns that a raucous stomping sounded from out the bar's side door, the surfacing shape tall and foreboding, with leathery skin and yolky eyes.

"What the hell?" Fink squealed. "Shit, now that can't be real." He pointed his gun at the corpse, finding the courage to defy its approach. "I—I heard about you, but come on, you ain't nothing but a myth, a freakin' fairy tale."

The Dead Sheriff fired his .45 straight at Fink's chest, knocking him from the bannister, down to the floor.

In a snap, Fuller fired in rebuttal, grazing the Sheriff's shoulder, but the corpse marched forth, turning from the end of the bar, reciprocating with two, steady blasts that struck the top of Fuller's brow.

The bleeding Fink struggled to stand, coughing and sputtering, his pistol half-cocked. He squeezed the trigger, but in his misguided zeal hit the dusty chandelier, a glob of unlit candles thudding to the floor.

The Sheriff sauntered toward the man and with a bowel-bursting voice bellowed, "This is your comeuppance, Ronald Fink. You killed a lawman. One will now kill you."

"Please, no, I beg of you," Fink blathered, but in a second, the Sheriff had planted a bullet into the man's brow, killing him.

The Sheriff turned, as folks finally found the courage to peek.

"Let that be a lesson to you all," the Sheriff gurgled through his unhinged mouth. "Kill a lawman—kill any man—and you will suffer the Dead Sheriff's wrath."

Two plump, bare-breasted women in black garter belts and undersized bloomers appeared above from Fink and Fuller's chamber. Upon sight of the living corpse, they screamed and bolted their jiggling derrieres back inside.

Sam relished the effect, yet noticed the Italian whore and her rosy-cheeked boss slipping into the shadows, their eyes filled with pronounced disgust.

Sam returned to the table, folded the posters and tucked them into his back pocket. He marched toward the swinging doors, leaving the Sheriff to stand stiff. Sam then poked his head outside and called, "O'Malley?"

Within seconds, the Irishman entered, looking sprightly and cool as he eyed the slain duo. "Good—that's done." He shot Sam a wary look. "Now, I trust you don't expect me to cart them out of here, do you?" He glanced at the Sheriff. "He's surely he's capable of handling the task."

Sam whispered, "I'd rather he move out on his own. We're his helpers. Folks need to realize that. I'll take one body, you the other. Share and share alike."

O'Malley sighed. "As you wish, Mister Cheveyo."

The bartender stumbled from the side and gave Sam an exhausted look. Sam detoured to the bar and slapped a stack of coins onto it.

"Thanks for playing along, barkeep. Trust me, the Sheriff is most appreciative."

"He's—he's not angry at me for not telling you they were upstairs?" The bartender's voice was cut with dread. "I was put in a terrible situation, you know, just terrible."

"Angry? Hell, no. I mean, sure you could have told me where they were from the start, but I realize that's not the way the game is played in good ol' Chesterfield. At least you didn't warn them we were here. You left that for those friendly shufflers. That was all I—or make that, the Dead Sheriff—needed for confirmation."

The man nodded, his gaze sparked with incredulity and relief.

Sam hopped away and yanked Fink by the cusp of his boots. O'Malley followed suit with Fuller, though Sam prompted the Sheriff to exit first, bestowing him a focused, no-nonsense gait as he strode into the sunlight.

As the corpses were dragged into the street, Sam noticed the old-timers huddled across the way, trembling and wondering if they would be singled out, but Sam saw no need. The Sheriff's presence was enough to teach them—and the rest of the town—an exemplary lesson. Of course, whether that lesson stuck for the long haul was another story.

"We'll drop them a few feet away," Sam instructed O'Malley, as the Sheriff slowed, and Chesterfield's own rangy lawman appeared, his uncouth moustache twitching with marked agitation.

O'Malley slid Fuller next to Fink and noticed the minacious tracks of blood the body had created.

"Perfect," Sam remarked, loud enough for the Chesterfield sheriff to discern and added with great relish, "I do hope we're not asked to take these bodies back with us."

"I don't think that should prove a problem," O'Malley added and turned to the fidgety lawman. "Are we correct in that my assumption, sir: that is, that we can collect the bounties here?"

Sam made the Dead Sheriff cock his Colt, which caused the Chesterfield lawman to cringe. Meanwhile, onlookers lined along the facades, whispering speculations as to whether the towering corpse was real or some imposing goon in a mask.

The Chesterfield sheriff edged his fingers to his lips, as if to nibble his nails, but then caught himself. "With all due respects, that goes against procedure, gentleman." His eyes bounced between O'Malley and Sam, in comedic unison with his sliding mustache, the Dead Sheriff's distasteful smell most likely the cause. "I'm, uh, I'm sure you understand. I'd be happy to help you load the carcasses onto your wagon if you'd like." He looked about. "I know it's around here somewhere. I did catch word of you having entered town, you see. Anyway, do feel free to point the way."

The Dead Sheriff gave his peer a disapproving groan, as sun rays skidded off his badge.

"I do believe," O'Malley rebutted, "that it is your job to tend to the bodies, Sheriff Masterson. The name is Masterson, is it not?"

"Yeah, um, Masterson, but you see, I'd have to haul the bodies all the way to Peach Water. That's nearly a two-day trip. I don't have the time to—"

O'Malley's eyes widened as he smiled. "Nor do we, Sheriff Masterson."

The lawman bit his lip.

The Dead Sheriff again groaned, his jaw this time unhinging. "Pay my men," the corpse commanded, bile spraying from the sides of his crumbling lips. "Pay them now."

The lawman regarded the cadaver's smeary orbs. "All right, All right. Very well." He yanked a wad of bills from his back pocket and handed them to O'Malley.

The Bostonian chuckled. "So, I see you were prepared." He counted the bills and waved the stack. "The right amount down to the last dollar." He packed the bounty into his vest. "It does dishearten me, though, that you wished to prolong the inevitable, though I'm not surprised, considering that you and the rest in this decrepit locale dared harbor these fugitives."

"F-fugitives? I had no idea they were even here, beyond some rumblings. Didn't have time to investigate, if the truth be known." Masterson squeaked a meek laugh. "I'm just glad you got 'em." He slapped his hip and wiped his brow. "Good riddance, too."

The Dead Sheriff snarled his disapproval, his stink mounting, making Masterson hop away, which in turn prompted laughter among the onlookers.

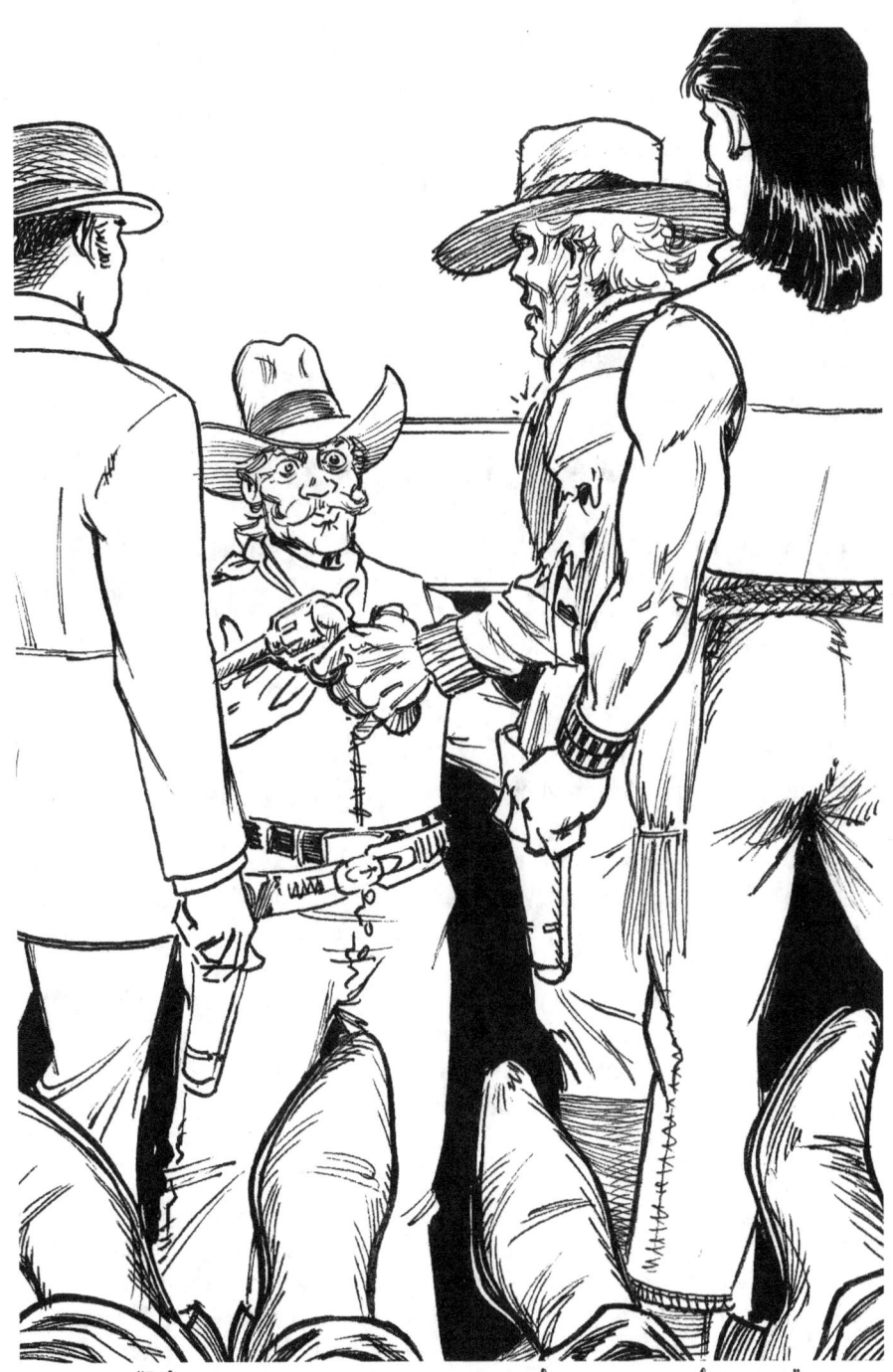

"That goes against procedure, gentleman."

O'Malley laughed with them. "Adios, my good lawman, and I do mean that in the most sardonic way."

Sam extracted the posters and tossed them atop the bodies. The Dead Sheriff then seized the lead, while Sam snatched the guns from the fallen. It was a habit he now practiced, for one could never have enough ammunition.

From there, the trio marched down a dingy side street, where their wagon had been looped to the side of a weathered shed.

With a spry sprint, Sam guided the Sheriff into his coffin, before joining the whistling O'Malley at the buckboard. In a flash, Sam then quickened the horses onward.

CHAPTER TWO

It was the sort of tepid day that most would call idyllic, except for the copious dust and buzzing flies. Perdifious sensed the atmosphere's bubbling apprehension as he oversaw the camp. His wide-brimmed hat shadowed the upper part of his calculating face, his body fixed straight upon his black mare, which like a good pet, mirrored his rigid introspection.

Perdifious's scars began to throb with a ruddy beat through his curly, black beard, his mediation deepening with a contemplative patience that cloaked his simmering impatience.

He replayed a sense-sparking reverie that had inserted itself into his brain over the past several days: a young Indian, a dandy and a standing corpse with a stench so righteous it made Perdifious wish to regurgitate, even if the entity was concealed from view.

A scrawny man in faded black approached on horseback and dismounted, gun aimed. The Indian and dandy poised themselves with discernible caution. Perdifious heard a shot, smelled the intermingling of smoke and decay, as the scrawny man hit the ground. The cryptic vision then faded, replaced by a burst of sibilating voices.

"A hint of the future," the demons hissed about his brain, "an unseen, consequential blossoming of unexpected, shifted seeds, if you will. The vision is but an inadvertent snag, not even intended at one point, but now raked for reality. The sky is changing, so is the air, tainted with something dark, something green, streamed by manipulated slime. You must absorb it all, Palmer Perdifious, fit one piece into the other, and settle your thoughts on the redefined present. It is only through that redesign and perhaps, just perhaps, if you seize the signs, you will gain the means to dispatch your win. .."

Perdifious nodded, refocused and watched his "general" gallop forth from the dust.

The man approaching was Vernon Walsh, the scrawny one in faded black whom Perdifious had dreamt of, a man with a damn, persistent need to please. Perdifious had recruited Walsh along the long, nomadic way, just as he had all his disheveled army, each man culled from a tumultuous time when most others engaged in a brother-against-brother war, spilling blood in honor of their foolish ideologies and pompous principles.

Walsh guided his horse alongside Perdifious's. He looked drained yet euphoric, as always so anxious to please.

"You might find this of interest, Mister Perdifious. That Dead Sheriff, he was seen—seen in full view of an entire town. The Indian was there with him, and some spectacled fellah. Anyway, two men dead in the trio's wake. The Dead Sheriff killed 'em in the saloon. The three collected the bounty before headin' out." He pointed west. "Right there in Chesterfield—right over the rim there."

Perdifious cocked his head. "Go on."

"Well, the way I found out is that a few of our men headed into Chesterfield this morn, just as you ordered, to snatch some supplies. The folks there can't stop talkin' about it. It's understandable, though."

"Any inkling where this trio may have gone—that is, are they headed our way?"

Walsh shrugged. "You'd probably know better than me, sir. You've got the insight." He smiled, but Perdifious's cold countenance sobered Walsh quickly. "They just left, is all. I reckon they couldn't have gotten far. Maybe if you concentrated, sir—"

"Don't tell me what to do." Perdifious's scars throbbed, his pupils turning ruddy. "I don't want that rank creature anywhere near me. You know that."

"All right, sir. Again, I only mentioned it because—"

"I don't need petty distractions, Walsh. I need a clear path with precise direction. That's one of your specialized duties, is it not? You stay abreast of the corpse's whereabouts, but only for good cause. I want to hear nothing of its existence, unless its presence is detrimental to our plans. In other words, if it appears to be on our heels, that it has our scent, then you tell me. I can focus on that kind of urgency. Another meager, distant visitation holds little weight or consequence. Understood?"

The downtrodden Walsh nodded and steered his horse back to camp, leaving Perdifious's focus flayed.

He ground his teeth and pounded his knee, for contrary to what he told Walsh, the agitating information was of value. The day of reckoning was near, but he need not panic. He need only to recognize the signs and perhaps, just perhaps, maneuver himself just enough to gain what he desired.

CHAPTER THREE

FROM THE JOURNAL OF RICHARD O'MALLEY:

Our elation has doused, though this is not so out of sorts. After any successful related kill and bounty, there comes a period of anticlimactic introspection.

But this time, the feeling runs much deeper.

Granted, the perception might be my own devise. I yet sense those vague peculiarities about the air: a proverbial calm before the storm, if one will.

Sam stays steadfast beyond his obligatory acknowledgment, pushing our horses at an even clip. We stop to eat, drink and sleep, replenishing ourselves for the grand intent of more circling and more bad men to strike. It is pure routine, and I would accept it without complaint, except for that aforementioned ambiance and that I have once more experienced the Dead Sheriff stirring during the night.

At first I thought it was Sam milling about, plagued by another spurt of the insomnia which we both endured more than we might care to confess. However, this noise was prompted by the canvassed-capped casket in the back, a practical, if not superfluous device that Sam had hammered together not long ago from some fresh boards we had come upon: nothing too fancy, but for whatever infernal reason, Sam deemed more "humane" for concealment sake than pinning the moldering occupant's limbs or stuffing him into some random confinement that was apt to collapse. I suppose he wanted to take care of his property, no more or less, but I suspect such care emanates more from an interred sentiment than practical maintenance.

Even so, the new structure might have proven more trouble than it is worth, for at least on that particular night it led to a persistent, hypnotic rapping within the Sheriff's panels. Without rhyme or reason, his knuckles played a haphazard tune that made me think of the most peculiar things, so that I imagined my wrists manacled and my back aching from great strain. What did it mean? Were these sensations but symptoms of my nocturnal dread, my continued pondering of whether the Sheriff harbored thought? If so, would that cognition define him as friend or foe?

Again, I do not know the extent of Sam's sorcery any more than he does. The Sheriff's rapping carried on for more than an hour, though Sam claims not to have heard it. He says that if it had, in fact, occurred, it was nothing but the result of the wind, a rubbing of branches from the tree under which we were stationed, perhaps even some inadvertent irritation elicited by our horses. Sam's surmise may be correct, but I know in my heart that something is amiss: that not only do I sense the air's riled ripples, but so does our gallant cadaver.

Perhaps evil attracts evil or at the very least, prepares for its inevitable advent.

Whatever the case, whatever the cause, I am cursed by my incertitude. Only time will tell if my dread is warranted or a mere figment of my suppressed regret.

An oddness brewed beneath its bannering blue, which was more than the bursts of dust and flies. Jake "Crabby" MacIntosh decided that whatever it was, it could be ignored. He had a more pressing task at hand: splitting wood.

The task was not for a need of firewood (spring had sprung early that year), and it was not because the exercise kept his frame chiseled (he was blubbery to a fault), but rather that it fueled a pounding furor.

He had been part of Perdifious's provisional army for more than two years, sometimes acting as a lookout and/or quasi (if not ornamental) bodyguard, but most often, one who kept all minor matters maintained. That meant he broke up fights and supplied women to the men, picking the prettiest for Perdifious upon those rare occasions when he did get the itch.

Getting women was not easy, though. Those willing required ample funds, and as much as his men had money to spare, it never seemed enough to cover the more intricate arrangements they desired. Such often led to arguments, scuffles and for those gals who refused to perform for free, death.

To sustain a reasonable supply—funds, that is, not women— he would take to the roads and adjacent paths, but those ventures were risky, considering folks were now more inclined to carry guns.

If the truth be known, Crabby disliked guns, and not for their killing potential. He didn't like their cumbersome feel; didn't even wear a holster for that matter. If he had an issue with some fellow, he settled it the old fashioned way or as his crass compatriots would state, "claw to claw."

And personal, physical altercations happened often, since he was the men's primary brunt of jokes. It was through such jesting that he had, in fact, earned his nickname.

He sported a heavy, red mane and matching beard, though on occasion the strands looked orange in the light, with the varying pigments complemented by his shell-white pallor. When he fought men, he chopped and clamped down on them, as opposed to punching. Indeed, the nickname suited him, but he also found it cruel: another example of the lack of respect he endured.

And so why not just move on, work on a ranch or farm where his diligence would pay off without all the scrapes and scuffs? The answer was complicated.

For one, Palmer Perdifious was a most charismatic sadist. He influenced tasks with remarkable ease, implementing an uncanny view of the past, present and future, which was damn impressive considering that few in their camp had ever worked, let alone flaunted menial social skills. Perdifious enticed all his leaguers with the galvanizing assurance of world conquest, which due to the man's cutthroat conviction, most believed would reach fruition, as long as patience prevailed. In the meantime, the higher a member's status in Perdifious's ranks, the greater the benefits. Sure, Walsh might be the current, designated, right-hand man, but Crabby was no slouch in the hierarchy, either. And still, there he was, splitting wood to work off his frustrations.

He split a large log, and with a huff, swung the axe onto his shoulder, feeling more placated though not entirely fulfilled. However, upon stepping to the side, he noticed a couple of brawny men fighting in the distance. It was, in truth, an organized slugfest, like so many that had come before, the sort of melee their leader endorsed, if only to let the men let off steam. Others were gathered around these brawlers, having created a makeshift ring, fueling the rule-less revelry with contemptuous cheers and jeers.

One of the brawlers hit the ground, mud splattering onto the one who stood. Laughter broke, spurring the apparent victor to kick the fallen in the head, which then ended the bout.

Crabby yawned, but the gesture hurt his jaw, rekindling his frustration and in the process of rubbing his neck to counterbalance the pain, a wavering cloud caught his eye. Funny thing. Was it a lion, insect or dragon? He chuckled at the fluctuating ambiguity, watching it adapt what became a set of large, puffy eyes.

"You lookin' at me, you sonnava bitch?" Crabby raised his hand and fanned his fingers. "That's right. Come on down. Let's see what yah got."

As if in response, the thing curled, its rear back arching, its four smoky appendages shuffling, phasing from whitish gray to a kind of stormy lime.

Lime (or more precisely, a vivid green) happened to be Crabby's favorite hue, since such reminded him of the sea, though the most he had ever seen of such was in paintings.

The pigment darkened.

"What the hell?"

He grew ever more concerned by the strange shifting, not so much because he thought it held sustenance, but that he feared he might be losing his mind. He seemed to decipher the apparition's cause, though he knew not how or why. This intuition implied a need to perform an extraordinary deed, but again how and why he could not say. Crabby only knew that the shape was beckoning him via some form of concentrated prayer, its intent malignant, maybe even vindictive. Such a peculiar thing for Crabby to fathom, but there it was, slipping into his mind like some prerequisite command.

The shape descended, swinging like a feather, but as it neared about ten feet away, it no longer looked as grand in scope and was perhaps even diminutive for its curious design.

It landed, at first rolling like a ball upon the grass, before snapping up with startling rapidity, fixing its pupil-less orbs upon Crabby.

Crabby nudged the axe from his shoulder and prepared for the worst.

With this, the gelatinous anomaly swung its head back, its neck bouncing like a coil and with attentive precision, stepped toward the man, wobbling like a marionette along the way.

Crabby placed the axe before his face.

"I don't want no trouble. Whatever you are, whatever you want, I can't help you, so you just let me be. Hear me? Let me be."

The creature paused and blinked its fuzzy eyes. It then held up its hands, spindly and oversized in comparison to its wrists. Though it had no lips, it opened its mouth and in a voice that was not male or female hummed, "I have an offer."

Crabby extended the axe in threat. "Offer? What the hell you mean, offer? What could you possibly offer me? What are you anyway? Some goddamn demon?"

The thing wobbled its head, implying contemplation. "Demon?" Its mouth curled. "So, you do know what I am."

Crabby's stunned silence gave the creature ample chance to explain, in a way that unfurled via avidity and evident rote:

"I come on behalf of the Master, a Moloch Junior, if you will, though I do realize that reference would hold little meaning for you. No matter. I've been summoned as the result of a distressed, distorted request, to give the methodology of enlistment a spirited twist. The Master has felt the vibrations of this vicinity through his subconscious intellect and knows the basic unrest and hunger that pervades the terrain. You, for one, are dissatisfied, but trusted by one who can take matters to the next level: that is, if he were persuaded to do so. Alas, all significant accomplishments occur in meticulous steps, never leaping to the line's end, for each participant is unique in his own disposition, desires and so on. In other words, no matter how keen one's insight, people do need convincing." The thing took a deep, raspy breath before adding, "The Master believes you can prompt the next phase based on the variables that have been dealt, that is, if you'd be so kind."

Crabby's head was spinning. He shrugged, but figured he might as well play along. "So, what's in it for me?"

The thing grinned. "Respect."

Crabby snorted. Had the freakish, little bastard read his mind?

"Sure, I could use some respect. Who doesn't? But I've already heard this con. Palmer Perdifious stuck it in my ear. What makes you—or this Master—any damn different?"

"Palmer Perdifious—ah, yes. He strives to be wicked, but the Master—oh, the great, monstrous Master—is rotten enough to the innate core to make good on any promise, as long as the precursor results benefit him."

The entity's glib phrasing struck Crabby as sincere.

"You may not realize it," the creature continued, "but you have the potential to climb higher within Mister Perdifious' ranks. That platform has been set for a decent spell, in fact. Your pompous Palmer Perdifious only needs the incentive. In other words, he needs to listen to you through me."

Crabby shook his head. "Nah, he won't listen, no matter who dishes it."

"Oh, but he will, for the Master will fill you with the magical, silver-tongued means. Perdifious yields power, the sort that can seize an item the Master desires, a special trinket that was stolen from him, though in fact, the thievery was twofold, with one item now having fallen to the wayside. So be it."

"Why don't you find this trinket yourself? You float among the clouds, don't you? Bet you see a lot from up there."

The creature sighed. "It seems my words have fallen on deaf ears. Let me rephrase the matter. I am but fluff, a dream, a flatulent transmission of green. I need eyes—veritable eyes—from which to see as any human would see. I need a body to inhabit." The creature absorbed Crabby's portly frame. "I need your strength, your girth, if you'd only lend it."

"So, that's your bullshit offer?" Crabby shook his head and his big belly along with it. "You want to take over my, uh, body?"

"Yes, and there's no need to fret over the merger. You'd still be you, but with all your best attributes accentuated. In this way, you would be all the stronger, all the wiser and more susceptible to the respect you so crave."

As preposterous as it sounded, the prospect intrigued Crabby, so much so that he lowered his axe, allowing the creature to creep closer.

"Do you consent, Jake MacIntosh? Will you let my essence merge with yours?"

Crabby was tempted, but unsure how to reply, and so the entity did what was only natural. It sprung forth, spreading its essence with full force into Crabby's flesh, flooding his mouth and nostrils with its bittersweet, netherworld goo.

Crabby gasped, coughed and laughed—laughed uproariously, in fact—his emotions thriving and riving until his angst, his deep-seated resentment, peaked like never before, his eyes seizing all that stretched before him.

From afar, another set of men had begun fighting. One hit the mud. How pathetic, Crabby thought, as the creature stole his vantage. Neither competitor could dare prove a match for him. Why not show these hapless fools a thing or two?

With axe grasped and knuckles protruding, he barreled forth, his flabby frame dancing in unison as he unleashed a wild, Scottish cry. Within seconds, he was upon the makeshift ring. Men turned, but all too late, for Crabby had swiped his blade into those who obstructed his path.

Heads flew from necks, fingers from hands, hands from arms.

Men shouted, some to the point of shrieking like little girls, as Crabby sprung into the centered brawlers, decapitating one and then the other, as a brave few leapt upon him from behind, punching, hammering, tearing into his back.

Crabby shook them off and again swung his axe, but this time it slipped from his hands. More men leapt in, but he swatted them away, clamping down on those nearest, crushing and squeezing their shoulders and necks until they merged with the mud.

Before long, he stood alone, panting with euphoria. He retrieved his axe, more than prepared to mutilate more if need be, but they were wise enough to hold their ground. He looked to the sky and guffawed with coarse gusto, until someone snuck from behind and tapped his shoulder.

With a blustering grunt, he swiveled.

Peridifous smiled as if in apology, for this was the first time he had sensed the wealth of Crabby's grandeur, but was it truly Crabby's? Something foreign seemed to stir within the portly man. Whatever it was, it was best to wheedle it.

"I'm not fond of you diminishing our numbers, Mister MacIntosh, but I certainly do relish your vigor. Impressive, indeed, and that scent— ah, most enticing. What is it?" Perdifious took a long, gluttonous sniff. "Whatever it is, it bleeds from your pores—a kind of lime, I would say." He motioned Crabby to follow. "To my tent, please. I would like to converse with you in private."

The flustered onlookers gurgled and chattered, transfixed by the ragged body parts strewn before them.

With great pride, Crabby marched behind his leader, his dripping axe braced upon his shoulder, his heart filled with anticipation.

The thing had, indeed, made him something more, something better, something stronger—something worthy of a dictator's ear. Perhaps now, he would gain the respect—and rank—he so justly deserved.

Crabby (or at least the quasi, altered impression of him) stood before Perdifious's small, oak desk, his pudgy fingers still gripping the axe. His leader regarded him with keen rumination as he rapped the desk top with focused intent.

"What prompted you to do this thing?" Perdifious asked, his grin taunting but favorable. "I don't mind impulsiveness, as long as it's within reason.

Please, do tell me."

Crabby shrugged, though he knew the reason. It was, of course, all due to the man he now regarded.

Perdifious rapped further. "Intuition tells me you've changed, and not through a mere spurt of madness. If Jake MacIntosh is no longer exclusive to the man who stands before me—and I do solemnly believe that is the case—how might I classify you?"

"A messenger, I suppose." Crabby felt a trickle of lime seep from his nose, and his confidence rose. "A messenger, for certain."

Perdifious considered the claim. "A messenger in what regard? For whom and what purpose?"

Crabby's demeanor stiffened per an inner command. "I come on behalf of a source far greater than any you have known—a source that, if it should so choose, could scour your mind and dissolve the demons of your youth with a mere click of his fingers. What stands before you is but one example of the miraculous, dark magic that he administers."

"So, Mister MacIntosh is a vessel for some sorcerer, but how...why?"

The big man blinked, as a trace of the old Crabby surfaced. "You have inspired me, Mister Perdifious. You have given me reason to rage. I grew tired of waiting, thinking of what was to be and when I looked to the sky, it sent this apparition to bless me. You know me; trust me, even if you don't respect me. Because of that, the thing gave me the chance to set matters right."

Perdifious sneered. "Go on."

"In truth, it goes beyond a man's simple hopes and dreams. It links to the undead lawman, his Indian compatriot, the one known as Cheveyo."

Peridifious bristled.

"Your caution is admirable, Palmer Perdifious, but if you evade the walking cadaver, you will never gain the victory you crave. The air smacks of your desire to wage war, to dispatch the first in what will be a limitless run. Alas, you fear the lawman's influence. You believe somehow, someway his presence is meant to impede you."

"Perhaps what you say is true, but what would you have me do to remedy it?"

"The Indian holds the key, an amulet to be precise. It wields sinister magic, but was stolen in the tricky thick of things. A reckless agent let the totem slip through his fingers, along with its instructional text, a powerful, spellcasting source, though the precious pendant remains the Master's unquenched desire. To say the least, the Master wishes it back."

"The Master?"

"Yes, the Master, one not unlike yourself, though spawned from a different end of the iniquitous spectrum. Because of his circumstantial confines, he must look to others to engage in the retrieval game. If you seize the amulet, he will grant your wish to rule on a more expansive plane than you ever imagined. The Master acknowledges that we each hold special talents. The Master has his. You have yours. Yours are well suited to perform a most essential means to an end. The Master has meditated on this matter for quite some time. He has felt the potent range of your presence, the vast, clairvoyant component of your imagination. He knows that you are up to the task: the right man for the job."

"How do I know this isn't a ploy?"

Crabby lowered his axe, as a brush of lime imbued his cheeks. "You know that I am sincere, for you see things far clearer than ordinary men. Again, I must stress that you are as unique as the Master, with a deft means to twist the variables. Nothing would please you more than to purge this earth of its virtues, to redefine it for no other reason than it can be done. There is no greater aspiration than that, Palmer Perdifious: cruelty for the sake of it, that is."

Perhaps, thought Perdifious, his vision of Walsh's death had been more than a by-chance burp. Perhaps, just perhaps, it was a small prelude to victory.

"Show me. Prove to me that the Master knows who I am and what I am capable of doing. Pull from my head something that distinguishes me, defines me, something important, perhaps full of dread, that only I would recognize."

Crabby motioned Perdifious toward him. "Very well."

Perdifious's eyes fixed on Crabby's, which sparked with pure, unfettered fury.

Light left the tent.

From out the consuming blackness, a vision took form, old in its surreptitious heart, bracketed by cruel, childish intent: a pivotal phase to rival even that of his founding night of flames.

"Show me. Prove to me that the Master knows..."

Newark, New Jersey 1842

Perdifious was thirteen, a resident of the doleful Newark Christian Orphanage, an obscure speck forty miles from Princeton. He had gone friendless for the entirety of his boring stay, though he did at least engage in basic communication. These exchanges grew terse at best, especially when asked how he had become scarred, which was as bad as when asked about his parents' impoverished descent and their ensuing suicide pact from poisoned tea.

As time passed, he had learned to don an apathetic guise whenever such inquiries came his way. The staff dismissed such indifference as his means of blanketing pain. To thwart his habit, they encouraged him to participate in as many activities as possible. For appearance sake, he only ever engaged such in a sideline manner, but when a request came to attend little Suzie Sommer's birthday party, he consented with uncharacteristic avidity.

The golden-curled Suzie was turning ten. Vibrant streamers had been strung throughout the dining hall to commemorate the event. Cake and ice cream were to be served, in addition to top-of-the-line cider.

Suzie had been decent to Perdifious (never having taunted him at least), and so to participate in her party seemed a gracious gesture. Besides that, Perdifious had a clever scheme in wait, one that he had fantasized over for quite some time and one that could prove a pivotal turning point in his adolescent life if successful. In this regard, he hoped the bottle he had snatched from the maintenance shed was not too conspicuous as it did bulge from his uniformed vest.

The owlish headmaster, Mister Hooten (who more than embodied his surname) noticed the boy milling outside the dining hall and found this odd, since Perdifious never roamed far beyond the boys' bed chamber. He adjusted his spectacles and cleared his throat. "I dare say, Palmer, is there something you want?"

Perdifious stiffened and shook his head.

"Then why are you here? You're not playing with matches again, I trust. Fire is never easy to harness," he explained with a tap to his cheek, "as you no doubt know."

Perdifious shrugged. "Agreed, sir, and I'm pleased to report that I've outgrown that pastime. At the moment, I only wish to assist with the festivities."

"That's admirable, Palmer, but the room is decorated. There's no more to do."

"Is the cake baked?"

"Mister Milton is commencing with it at this moment. It will be done before long, nice and hot, with cool frosting on top. You must be patient, my lad."

"I would like to help with the cake, if you don't mind."

"Again, that's admirable, Palmer, but Mister Milton doesn't need help. Now, be a good lad and run along."

At this point, Nurse Conroy entered, looking as pretty as a picture, the raven-haired apple of most orphaned boy's eyes, though Perdifious found her a vapid wench and knew she flaunted her perfumed charms only to gain special favor, such as by departing early on any given day.

"What did I hear?" she asked, giving Perdifious an affectionate glance.

"Young Palmer wishes to help Mister Milton finish Suzie Sommer's cake."

Nurse Conroy looked pleased. "I think that's a wonderful idea."

Hooton groaned. "Really, Nurse Conroy. Mister Milton doesn't need any help. He's on a tight schedule as it is. Any distraction would slow him down."

The nurse raised her bosom and pulled Hooten close enough to purr in his ear. Perdifious could hear her utter the names of the administrative staff, including the know-it-all Father Pringle, who had been the prime advocate of Perdifious's participation in the home's activities.

Hooten nodded, as beads of impassioned sweat rolled from his brow. "Very well, Beth—I mean, Nurse Conroy, though I must converse with Mister Milton first to make certain he doesn't mind."

Hooten departed, but within seconds returned, smiling more at his curvaceous nurse than the patient Perdifious.

"Mister Milton has given his blessing." He then shot Perdifious a stern glance. "Nevertheless, young man, you are not to get in his way. You listen to Mister Milton. Abide by his rules."

"Thank you, sir. I am most grateful."

Hooten opened the dining-room door, permitting Perdifious passage. The kitchen waited at the far end.

Perdifious skipped through, appreciating the plentiful spread of inviting dishes and bowls upon the sprawling table, whistling up an obstreperous storm as he approached the disgruntled Mister Milton, who peered from out of his hot chamber.

The big man's mustache flapped, as his belly extended under his floured apron. "Thanks for nothin', son. Truly, I've more than enough to worry about than you. Mister Hooten can be such an overbearing clout and well, I suppose the less said the better."

To taunt the big man, Perdifious spun on his heels. "If you want, I'll leave. I'm certain Mister Hooten won't be too pleased."

Mister Milton grabbed the boy by his collar and swung him around. "Hold on there, you rascal. No need to be hasty." He ushered Perdifious next to a big bowl and slipped a wooden spoon into his hand. "Stir that dough."

Perdifious complied with great vigor, enough to calm the baker who then yawned, sensing an opportunity to snooze. Upon a stool he plopped and braced his back against the wall.

Perfect, thought Perdifious, so perfect that fate had surely intervened.

From his pocket, he yanked the bottle and held it to the gaseous light, admiring its creepy skull and crossbones, but even more so, its crimson proclamation: CAUTION, CYANIDE FOR PESTS: CONCOCTED TO KILL.

With a wee whistle, he unscrewed the top, poured the contents in and returned the bottle to his vest. He then stirred some more.

When he thought the batch had gained the ideal texture, he recommenced his whistling.

Mister Milton snorted and opened his eyes. "Good God. Stop that infernal noise."

Perdifious hushed and hoisted the pasty spoon as if it were a trophy. "I do believe I'm done, sir."

"I'll be the judge of that." The baker waddled from the stool, stuck his finger into the bowl and licked a smidgeon. "Hmmm. Not bad. Not bad at all." He patted Perdifious's shoulder. "Good job, young man. Excellent, I must say."

"Thank you, sir. I did my best, don't you know?"

Perdifous then skipped away, returning to the boys' bed chamber to meditate before the dinner bell rang.

When such occurred, the children gathered in single file and took their seats. For a time they did no more than sip their water and picked at their beef, anxious for their ice cream, cider and cake.

Looking a tinge under the weather, Mister Milton wheeled out the latter: a large, triple-stacked mound with pink frosting and ten long, enflamed, spiraled candles.

Perdifious watched the flickers with insightful glee and even took a moment to savor the childhood event that had "scarred" him.

Mister Hooten and Nurse Conroy soon appeared, as Mister Milton granted Suzie a respectful bow and with a flamboyant wave, awarded Perdifious acknowledgment: "To my honorable helper, Palmer Perdifious, who stirred a most excellent batter. May you now all enjoy this delicious cake to mark our sweet Suzie Sommers's tenth birthday."

The children clapped. Suzie gave Perdifious an appreciative wink and blew out the candles.

Mister Milton sighed in weariness and then departed, while a group of bonneted ladies entered and poured the cider and scooped the ice cream into bowls. This left Mister Hooten to cut the cake, and Nurse Conroy to pass the plates.

The orchestration was quick and nimble, the children digging in with ravenous glee, except for Perdifious, who knew better.

Suzie pouted at her somber friend. "Why aren't you eating, Palmer?"

Nurse Conroy overhead and patted his head. "You should, Palmer. You did help make the cake, after all. It does look inviting." Nurse Conroy took a small chunk and slipped it past her pouty lips. "Tasty, indeed," she cooed. "Quite delicious, in fact."

Perdifous watched them all gobble, the collective gluttony exceeding his wildest dreams. He only had to wait until—

"I don't feel so well," said Suzie, bracing her tummy.

"Me, too," groaned a prepubescent lad, as another shot frantically for the corner.

"Oh, my," Nurse Conroy exclaimed, wobbling toward the latter as he regurgitated.

"What is this, now?" Mister Hooten declared, his words muffled by the children's whines. The servers scrambled about, tense and confused.

With marked calm, Perdifious slinked from his chair, a strange and conspicuous move which caught Hooten's eye.

"Where are you going, Palmer?"

Perdifious ignored the inquiry and continued toward the door.

"Come here, I say."

Mister Hooten began to follow, but then paused, his fingers clenched. He hobbled backward and held his chest, causing squeals from the frightened children.

Perdifious smiled and entered the long, dim hall, the muffled calamity warming his ears. He reached the orphanage's front entrance, opened its huge doors and with great mirth skipped into the autumnal air.

But now that he had brought his dream to fruition, where would he go?

He kicked through the pretty leaves. Did it matter? As the situation stood, he was free, with the world wide open for whatever he should so choose, give or take.

And on this optimistic note, his reverie began to fade, sealed as it was on a high, selfish note, but Perdifious's vision was never that concise, let alone one prompted by ghostly goo. They always rolled with related ideas, branching into other times and places.

He felt himself grow taller, his clothes changing with the passing seasons, his threads growing blacker, more intimidating.

Into secluded spots, he envisioned himself, making camp wherever he could, tackling menial jobs along the way, stealing from the downtrodden trails. Others of his unethical ilk joined him at times, only then to press on, leaving yet others to take their place: the process creating an unending cycle.

Like the fabled Robin Hood and his Merry Men, he and his varied troops stashed themselves among the woods, in caves and abandoned cabins, constructing plans for conquest while South broke from North, as brother fought brother in a bloody, overdrawn war.

Let the weak die, he thought. May only the strong survive. From the strong he would select his recruits, no matter which side they had embraced, building an army like no other.

Onward, his legs carried him, his swagger growing more confident, merging with the extending, anguished atmosphere, his scars more pronounced, more intuitive, but as superb as the callous culmination was, it fell short. He needed something more, something diabolical to the core.

It was only a matter of what fiery poison would rival the orphanage deed.

But as much as his dark heart yearned for some grand, abhorrent sequel, he could not shake the presence of the tall, rotted shape that waited in the murky distance, nor the Indian or the fancy-garbed gent who accompanied the thing. Try as he may, he could not fathom the corpse's cause, only that it, along with its faithful companions, remained an ineffable anomaly that somehow, someway would thwart him, unless he beat it to the punch.

Perfidious woke fresh and focused, assured by the Master's remote influence. Still, he felt the need to ask, "Can you assure me that I will face no harm, if I should accept this task, that no outside obstacle will intervene or harm me?"

Crabby raised a "claw" and flattened the other upon his chest. "I assure you, Palmer Perdifious, no harm will come to you, as long as you keep your eye on the prize. You only need to expand your mind to find that prosperous path. With it, your enemies will not gain the upper hand, and if—and when—you succeed, you will fulfill your life's mission: all that your guardian demons have promised."

"Then, I will consent to the deal. I will—"

An eruption of lime splattered him, and once upon his skin, it turned vivid violet, matching his meandering scars. He licked the residue, swallowing it shamelessly.

The Master's agent clapped his claws. "Wonderful, wonderful. I now grant you the means to seal the deal, a Faustian exchange not unlike the one you forged as a child. It will further expand the special insight you possess, allow you to see as never before, remember as never before. It will guide you, and you in turn will guide the Master to his revered medallion."

CHAPTER FOUR

O'Malley sat alongside his friend, a few feet from the wagon, on a bed of rocks, the Sheriff's cloaked casket visible under moonlight. In an odd way, the sight gave comfort, a sense of protection.

"That whole area unsettles me, Sam, and it's no wonder. That horrid, Texan town of Damnation chilled me to the bone. I don't care if a new one has replaced it. If it stands in the same spot, or even thereabout, it's tainted. I don't care how many alleged Bible-thumpers have settled upon its soil. Bad is bad, Sam."

Sam groaned. "We need to cover the circumference. It's part of the rotation, how we make our steady dollar. We'll break the cycle only when it feels right. It's as simple as that. We need to sustain ourselves, O'Malley. This is the only way to do it."

O'Malley growled "Sure, Sam, sure. The thing is, I keep thinking that our venturesome ways will run their course. Our fortune could run out, you know. I've been thinking of this for a good spell now. Sooner or later—"

Sam stood; his expression terse. "Enough gibberish, O'Malley. To question matters is to jinx them. You don't want our good fortune to slip, do you? We need to keep moving, keep circling—keep making good."

O'Malley glanced at the casket. "So, we're doing good, Sam?"

Sam bristled. "Yes. Look how many outlaws we've taken down."

"Through the help of a corpse."

"Your point?"

"The magic—how malleable, how trustworthy is it? Consider the source, Sam. Consider the fiend who wants it back."

"I do the magic as I see fit. Do you know why the Master disapproves, the real reason he wants the amulet back? Because I do good with it. The three of us do good. That's why."

Sam's proclamation surprised O'Malley. Sam had never made such a staunch stand before, having always displayed a practical indifference at best.

"On the surface, Sam, yes, I get your argument, but is it God's way? Is it God's will?"

Sam grimaced and then cursed under his breath, before barging off.

"Sam, I'm sorry. I didn't mean to strike a chord. I was only conjecturing, no more or less, my friend."

Sam remained silent as he looked to the stars: nothing fancy, just bland, judgmental eyes, spewing a steady, understated mockery.

After a spell, he glanced back at O'Malley, who had bowed his head as if in prayer. Was he asking for forgiveness? Why? Were the doctored-up tales he documented not meant to inspire good? The legend of the Dead Sheriff and his companion, Cheveyo had reached far across the land. Many now hesitated before committing any bad deed in fear that a living corpse might strike them down. There was no doubt good in that. A lot of good.

And yet Sam could not deny those murky spurts that made him question his intent as much as O'Malley did. There were those times when, as much as he refused to admit it, he wished he could flee the black magic.

In this regard, though his link to the Dead Sheriff may have proven effortless, it also felt forbidden. He could taste the bitter sweetness of its rot. There were times when he even wished to unravel the gamut of the Sheriff's mind—if the thing even had a mind. Sam operated the corpse from the outside looking in, making it walk and talk, pulling its strings to kill. It was Sam, therefore, who did the good, or was it rather the bad?

If only he could better understand the causes and effects of it all, he might be more at ease with the arrangement. And perhaps, just perhaps, that was why he insisted upon wandering. Wandering did not require contemplation. It allowed one to avoid the truth, and as much as he claimed to desire and respect it, the truth scared him.

Ashamed and confused, he curled himself into the grass and closed his eyes. For the rest of the night, it was best not to think of it. Tomorrow, though, was another story.

CHAPTER FIVE

Walsh suspected his leader had something stored up his sinister sleeve. Perdifious had talked about the neighboring towns, which ones were fortified and which were not. That, in itself, conveyed a burgeoning plan.

Purity seemed of most interest to Perdifious: a flimsy sanctuary overseen by Winifred Wakefield, who according to popular belief, had learned of Damnation's demise (as well as that of its fickle founder, the spurious Reverend Ludlow Skaggs), and in lieu (and perhaps in spite) of that town's notorious debauchery, had erected a replacement based on his veritable Christian creed. Its inhabitants did not believe in violence and therefore, banished guns, along with other "sinful" contrivances from their settlement. The group would be easy to conquer, but if so, why bother? Perdifious did, after all, cherish a challenge. Purity offered none.

"They harbor a philosophy," the disparaging guru explained, pacing within his tent, fingertips pressed. Crabby stood nearby, which struck Walsh as peculiar. Why keep this buffoon available, especially after that purposeless rampage? "Their message is strong and the pastor advocates the spread of virtue and piety. He claims that such will inspire similar towns to take root. What better way to demonstrate evil's might than to dismantle this man's symbolized optimism?"

Walsh still did not see the point and slipped a yawn.

"Am I boring you, Mister Walsh?" Perdifious's scars screeched through the webbed strands of his sinister beard

Walsh cringed and cursed his carelessness. "Oh, uh, I'm not bored, Mister Perdifious, not in the least."

"Good, I am glad to hear, because I do wish you to be the one to descend upon this town, the one to administer its slaughter."

"Slaughter?" Surely, Perdifious must be joking. "Purity, you say, sir?"

"Yes, I wish you to initiate its defiling. The purest of the pure do deserve an apocalyptic demise. And this extermination should be so complete, so grisly, as to exceed mere rumor or heresay. To ensure the monumental massacre, you will take to this town a handpicked brigade—a dozen of our finest and cruelest should do. You, my faithful general, will act as my official conduit. I will see what you see, as the men follow your example." Perdifious smiled. "Are you up to the task, Mister Walsh?"

Walsh twitched and in so doing, glanced at Crabby. The man's conspicuous roundness now made him look more aristocratic than clownish.

"I'll go, sir, but MacIntosh should go with me. He's got more than enough fight in him to cover ten men, with or without that damn axe."

"A wise choice, but Mister MacIntosh's services are not required for this mission. He will remain at my side for the sake of counsel."

The flabbergasted Walsh nodded. "When do I depart, sir?"

"This hour is as good as any. You'd arrive in Purity by Sunday morn: an ideal time to make your presence known."

The request spooked Walsh, but he forced a smile in spite of it. "All right, I'll get the men. We'll head out by hour's end."

With this, Walsh exited, wasting no time to comb the camp for his finest and cruelest, many of whom were still stunned from Crabby's attack, but perhaps all the more eager because of it. The prevailing edge was good. It would ensure the job would get done.

All the same, the men filled Wash's ears with questions, but he only promised a substantial, immoral reward if they followed through. After all, he had no idea how he might conduct the assigned slaughter. He only knew that it had to be done and that to please Perdifious, it had to be huge. Now that he was an "official conduit"—whatever the hell that meant— he would not to let the bastard down, let alone grant satisfaction to that pompous pile of blubber who dared rob his respected rank.

CHAPTER SIX

FROM THE JOURNAL OF RICHARD O'MALLEY:

Sam said little as we journeyed the next morn, which gave our ride a bout of slow, pensive irritation. He often took a pretty pass or two before getting back on track. Perhaps these idyllic tangents were his way of mollifying the evident agitation, but if so, the long-term effects failed.

Something is, indeed, bothering him, and far more than earlier: a resurfacing of a tremulous glint, which goes beyond our quarrel.

I asked Sam to stop the wagon so that I might relieve myself. Upon my return, I insisted that he detail his concern, despite the risk of extending our dispute. To my surprise, his response was relaxed, at least enough so that he articulated, "I'm fearful. I sense the gloom. I've sensed it for some time now, just like you. Travelling in circles has been my way of avoiding the obvious, I guess. I see that now. I do believe something bad is going to happen."

After this appreciated but cryptic confession, he leapt from the buckboard and paced.

I asked that he elaborate further, but he refused. At most he suggested that we get plenty of rest and continue our backroad ventures in the morn. I did not object, since the outskirts did prove more pleasing to the eye than those banal, main trails.

However, with ample time on my side, I decided to review my journal to make my marginal notes, leaving Sam to toil from view. I presumed he was assessing his confiscated guns, but after a spell, I sensed otherwise and headed to the wagon's rear. There I saw him standing before the exposed casket, where the Sheriff sat straight as flies buzzed about his crown.

It was no more or less than that, but their perplexing eye-to-eye stance felt more foreboding than contemplative, enough so that I tapped Sam's shoulder and asked, "Are you all right?"

Sam stirred, thus prompting the Sheriff to fall back. He then covered the corpse, remarking that he did not wish to wait any longer, that we should press on at that moment.

I did not question the particulars and perhaps for privacy's sake, I should not commemorate any of it here (though I could remove any such segment during revision). Still, I cannot ignore Sam's ominous progression. There is no doubt that his state of mind could impact our welfare.

CHAPTER SEVEN

Walsh took a swig from his bottle of bourbon, his courage swirling as his men waited, their horses clopping in place. They had been waiting over an hour now at Purity's fringe. Perdifious had implied that he would be watching in the wings, that he would know their every move and therefore, Walsh's execution of attack had to be perfect or thereabout.

"I was here before," one of the men remarked, tapping the bruised upper eye he had gained from Crabby's assault. "This is where that Damnation town was. Real big place. Good gambling. I remember it well—miss it much."

"Shut the hell up," Walsh snapped, taking another swig. "I'm tryin' to concentrate."

"On what?" asked another, rubbing his bruised lip, another badge of

Crabby's fury. "We're gonna round 'em up, right, Mister Walsh? What's so hard bout that?"

Walsh shook his head. "We don't have to round 'em up. It's Sunday morn, goddamn it. If it's Sunday morn, they'll go to church. This is one of those religious towns. The little angels will flow to the same spot. That makes it easier."

The church bell rang.

"Ah, there we go—at long last." Walsh finished his bottle and threw it to the ground, then steered his horse downhill. "Follow my lead, men. You'll know what to do when the time comes."

Irrepressible joy (and maybe some wee, humble pride) filled Winifred Wakefield's heart. He took a deep breath and listened to the bell's robust, sanctified christening.

This Sunday was important—six months to the day that they had staked their foundation upon this once spoiled land. To Wakefield, the accomplishment was nothing short of a miracle and indisputable proof of the Lord's vast virtue.

He now stood outside his temple, not far from its wee, side cemetery. A handful of men and women were buried in it: individuals who had perished soon after arrival, weighed as they were from the weariness that accompanies long miles and old age.

The pale-blue sky blanketed the cross-spiked expanse. He savored it all from the church's rear platform. Such a lovely Sunday and to think that within this very proximity there had reigned such debauchery. The wind had swept the town's charlatan leader and the rancid remnants of Damnation away, for the wind was an instrument of the Lord, and the Lord would never let evil flourish for long. That was for certain, as he and his people had proven.

Wakefield removed his wide-brim hat and fanned his face. It was getting hot. A man as frail and aged as Wakefield—a man who had remained married solely to his work and vision—had to sustain his strength. His flock expected it of him. He was honored to oblige. It was his honed style, his modest, hard-working creed.

He had progressed from one unassuming locale to another over the years, a young man who had lent his services when the stationed shepherds fell ill or pursued theological sojourn. During each sermon, each act of charity, he saw what lay before him: a growing denomination, graced by humility. Humility remained his predominant trait and because of this, he never failed to lure new members, combing towns that had no churches along their stage-coached path, bringing the mystified and heartbroken along for the ride. It all led to this—this glorious town called Purity.

"Hello, sir," John Brown called, tipping his hat, his wife, Josephine, and little daughter, Cindy, with him, both bonnet-clad and beaming. "We're anxious to hear this morning's sermon, Pastor."

"I am honored to give it, Brother John, and especially on such a lovely May day, albeit a warm one."

"Amen," said Brown, with a tip of his hat. "Warm but delightful. Praise the Lord."

The family trailed toward the church's entrance, as more parishioners flooded in from various points, offering their gracious greetings to the pastor.

By the time they converged within, the bell had hushed. Wakefield closed his eyes and thanked the Lord for the opportunity set before him. He was filled with the spirit and stepped through its rear entrance, like an actor headed for the stage.

The spectacled and silver-haired Miss Petula Preston pedalled a warbled, if not indiscernible hymn on the organ. Such a sweet sound, thought Wakefield, for it cradled imperfection within perfection, representing the common folk at their most modest and exemplary capacities.

He placed his hat on the pulpit and gave Miss Preston a respectful nod. He looked into the packed pews, at his parishioners' bright, eager faces.

Miss Preston lifted her fingers with playful panache, signaling completion.

Wakefield chuckled. "Thank you, Miss Preston, for supplying this morn's prelude music. We look forward to you recommencing later, at which point we will join you in song."

Miss Preston beamed, while the pudgy, tight-suited bell ringer, Kurt Swift, appeared from the side door and squeezed into the front pew, giving a respectful tap to his brow.

Wakefield returned the gesture with fondness. "It's been a long road; my good people, but not without satisfaction, as hard work often proves." Wakefield spread his arms and rolled his eyes upward. "Praise Jesus Christ, our great and compassionate Lord." He then looked down, focusing on his Bible, but instead of opening it, he projected a divine glow.

"Today, this hallowed Sunday, I would like to praise you—each and ev-

"We're anxious to hear this morning's sermon..."

ery one of you—for each member gathered here symbolizes the power of God's virtue. You have done what some claimed could not be done: traveled through the limitless, burdensome elements and upon arrival, built a town from scratch in no less than six months—six amazing months." His sky-blue eyes twinkled. "You did this without devilish drink or ghastly guns, without government aid, the intervention of masked crusaders or—and do pardon the macabre levity this may invoke—an alleged, walking corpse with a badge." Wakefield suckled a snicker, though some of his flock did laugh. "Oh, yes, my friends, we've heard all sorts of rumors about all sorts of hollow magic. Nevertheless, we have not once turned our eyes from God's sweet purity. And so with this humble acknowledgment, we have come to call our salt-of-the-earth town Purity. It now stands as our heartfelt, little Heaven on Earth."

The parishioners smiled with satisfaction, but more so, admiration for the man who had led them to their gracious success.

"And this little Heaven on Earth, my good people, will be shared with anyone who wishes to partake: a pattern for other such towns to take root. We shall spread Purity's influence through acts of kindness, forgiveness and empathy—each of us personifying Christ's methodology with each daily step, with each wayward stranger we meet."

A barrage of enthusiastic amens circled, but no sooner had they been uttered, a fierce thundering of hooves, capped by crass laughter, was heard from outside. .

The ruckus startled Wakefield but he found enough mettle to keep his calm. Had he not often told this flock not to fear? Whoever was approaching was welcome. However, his people looked uncertain.

A man bellowed from behind the doors, "They're in there all right. I'll head in first, warm 'em up."

Wakefield cleared his throat and did his best to look undaunted. "We will show compassion in the face of adversity. We will let resentment and contempt bleed away, no matter how bitter it may be." His face turned whiter. "We will accept our enemy, no matter what circum—"

Walsh flung open the doors, and with him came an unsettling wind, warm and stifling, along with enough dust to make the congregation cough.

The scrawny invader looked about, his face wracked by frenetic inebriation. "Why, now, what do we have here? If it ain't another gatherin' of the sheep." Walsh raised his pistol. "Hypocrites—one and all. That's what you are."

The parishioners looked to Wakefield for clarity. Surely, he would supply guidance, a few profound words to dispel this audacious outburst.

Wakefield folded his hands. "Surely, you do not mean that, good sir. We are not hypocrites. As I was just telling those gathered, we accept all who come into our fold and ostracize none, whether they accept our creed or not. It is our way."

Walsh laughed so hard that the pews appeared to spin before him. "You must be out of your holier-than-thou head, old man. You know what? You're just another prophet of fuckin' lies." He waved his gun about, causing the audience to gasp and squirm. "You could care squat about my kind. That goes for all of you here. You don't care that my kind's been stepped on, ridiculed, deprived by your likes for centuries. It's become a damn, sickening routine among you high and mighty sorts, and its time the tables were turned."

It was then that Wakefield realized the danger before him. If he could not persuade this man from doing them harm, what would the consequences be? Would prayer be enough to settle any of it?

"Hypocrites, hypocrites, hypocrites, "Walsh continued with a sloppy jig, "You ain't worth the salt of my piss. Look at you goddamn fools, shaking like leaves. Where's your God now?" He cocked his pistol. "How strong is he? Strong enough to stop a bullet?"

Wakefield's heart pounded. Fear, not faith, gripped him. "Enough. I beg you, sir, put down your weapon. Let these people be. Repent—repent before you do something rash. Repent before you do something you'll regret."

From beyond the open doors and through the swirling dust, Wakefield saw men dismounting: dirty, scarred and tattooed, raw contempt searing in their heartless eyes.

Walsh grew cockier with their approach. "I'll ask again, preacher man. Your God strong enough to stop a bullet?"

Wakefield seethed in a way that was uncharacteristic of him. "Strong enough to stop a devil like you, sir."

Walsh's eyes bulged with surprise, and with this he felt the sensation that someone else peered through them. "Do tell, now," he sputtered, trying to sustain his control. "How 'bout we test that theory, padre?"

Wakefield trembled as Walsh spun on his heels, firing at Miss Preston's bosom and no more than a second later, splattering the stunned Swift, who had run to her side, only then to fall hard to the floor.

Screams rocked the church. The wild-eyed brigade pranced in a monstrous wave, some with pistols, others with rifles, firing in fast, mad abandon, striking down men, women and alas, children, all in one bullet-sprayed swoop, cursing and hooting the whole sadistic while.

Frantic, the Browns squeezed beneath their pew, shielding their little girl, pleading her to not whimper, to stay quiet, but their request was unconvincing beneath the rumbling, wooden framework. Cindy elicited a muffled spurt and felt the thrust of the bullets pound her parents' backs, the air snuffed from their lungs.

Wakefield suckled the unfurled carnage, his fellow assailants reloading and firing again and again and again, even upon the defunct bodies, while cutting off those few who yet sheltered themselves or dared to escape, blowing off the back of their heads in the process.

Wringing his hands, Wakefield chanted, "Repent, repent, repent," which only prompted Walsh to hunker toward the pulpit. "What's that, shaman?" The bad man cupped his ear and raised his gun. "Repent? Is that what you said?"

Wakefield choked on his chant and with this meek gesture, his faith faltered, his will to live vanquished.

"Maybe you're the one who should repent, preacher man." Walsh cocked his trigger, his mind—tied with impenetrable might to Perdifious—imploding with the unparalleled, poisonous thrill to kill. "Best leave this earth with your soul nice and clean, don't yah think?"

Walsh's bullet struck Wakefield's brow dead center, hurling the man past his pulpit, his hat sailing upward only to land like a plucked feather upon his defeated face.

In his final seconds, the pastor hoped beyond hope for some ethereal light to take him away, to reverse the heinous process he had witnessed, but instead he found only a gut-wrenching darkness calling, and in that darkness, his soul slipped, anchored by unabashed hate.

From out of her parents' dead weight, Cindy wrenched herself free, crawling to the outer aisle. She saw the side door, from where Mister Swift had entered, inconspicuous enough for a quick getaway.

She tiptoed around the sprawled bodies and slid across the streaming blood, doing her best not to cry or faint.

She exited into the blinding sunlight, which beat down upon her curly crown, punctuating the pure hellishness of what she had experienced.

She yanked loose her bloodied bonnet, tossed it to the swarming dust and taunting flies, walking as fast as she could across the endless grass. The profane whooping of the invaders still filled her ears, as the wind shoved her ever onward.

When the town of Daisy Fields emerged within the haze of dusk, Cindy only then felt compelled to scream—a scream so intense that the town's inhabitants had no choice but to rush forth and find her.

CHAPTER EIGHT

FROM THE JOURNAL OF RICHARD O'MALLEY:

Sam claims he hears the rush of horses, the battle cries of men. I suppose this stems from his Indian instinct, for I hear only the roll of our wheels.

We will not reach Purity within our estimated timeframe. That makes little difference to me. What are a few hours, a few days more? We will arrive at our destination soon enough, obtain what bounty information we can (if any) and then move on.

I wonder if I should still embrace my somber path. I will need to give the matter serious consideration, considering Sam's current mindset.

If he is plagued by woe and becomes unfocused on the cause, I fear this could hamper his manipulation of the Sheriff. By no means would that work to our advantage. I would not wish to fall victim to that result, disloyal though that may make me sound.

Walsh rode as blood dried upon his clothes, whipping his horse to the point of abuse, the poor creature snorting and spitting every speck of the way.

Perdifious came into view, along with his queue-layered entourage, his stance high and assured, his eyes locking with Walsh's, as their mental overlap faded.

Walsh realized his leader would expect elaboration, though for no other reason than habit's sake. The man's tight countenance spoke omniscient volumes in that regard, as did Crabby's, albeit more through steely nonchalance than intuitive projection.

Perdifious waited for Walsh to guide his horse alongside his, smirking in such a way that his incisors shined. "Quite a flamboyant display, Mister Walsh. Fascinating what liquor and a pity-me attitude can provoke. Nevertheless, you did prove an ideal conduit, if not a garrulous one."

Considering what he had accomplished, Walsh took offense, but dared not express it.

"I take it your men will clear out the bodies."

"They'll dig a ditch, toss 'em in. It'll take some time to purge the church."

"I'm certain they'll do as well as they can. For what it's worth, I don't mind the smell of blood. Paint is paint."

Crabby laughed.

Walsh gave his rival a sour glance.

"In any event," Perdifious continued, "I am sorry you traveled to meet us halfway, but the impulse was more yours than mine. Still, for dramatic effect, it benefits those who did not engage in the slaughter. Your presence confirms that we now have a permanent base. On the other hand, what's ever meant to be permanent, eh, Walsh?" He gave his henchman a scrutinizing squint. "But thanks to your efforts, we also have a sordid tale to spread. Hmmm. That might be an honorable task for you. What do you say? You willing to spread the good word?"

Walsh got the disrespectful hint. "Sure, I can do that. Where do you want me to start?"

"I'll leave that to you. There are plenty of towns, plenty of saloons, plenty of opportunities to inform people that Purity is under new management."

"That kind of word might also get you unwanted visitors."

"If you mean bad men, the more the merrier, Mister Walsh. We do need our legion to expand, especially after Mister MacIntosh's abrupt purge."

"I was referring to marshals, bounty hunters and the like, sir."

Peridifous rolled his eyes. "They're equally welcome. The question is, once they're in our midst, what's the best means to mutilate them?" He winked.

The men within hearing snickered, with Crabby leading that charge, his cheeks now as red as his hair. After a spell, Perdifious raised his hand, snuffing the guffaws, for it was evident that the pinched-face Walsh had more to say.

"I take it, you'd prefer I spread the word now—at this very minute, Mister Perdifious?"

His eminent mentor offered another squint. "One good deed deserves another, does it not, Mister Walsh? Besides, the blood on your clothes, though somewhat obscured by their lackluster pigment, will get the word rolling, give your claim credibility, that is."

Walsh forced a smile and without pause directed his horse east, while Perdifious signaled his entourage toward Purity.

"Anything you can tell us, dear? Anything at all?"

Cindy sat on a stool near Sheriff Paul Kendle's desk. He was concerned, but also frustrated. He glanced at his wife, Emily, figuring a woman's touch might inspire articulation.

"She's frightened, Paul," the little, silver-haired lady said, "agitated to the point of having grown numb. Look at her clothes. It's not just dust and dirt." She whispered from the side of her mouth. "Those are blood stains. You can even smell it on her. Oh, the poor thing's been through something horrific, Paul."

"I see that, Emily, but I can't do much without knowin' the reason." He knelt, letting the child get a good view of his stern, hawkish face. "It's okay, darlin'. We just want to help. Now, you were screaming when you came to town and shaking like a leaf. Something clearly scared you. Now, what was it, dear?"

She remained quiet, her stare unswerving.

Kendle cocked back his hat and rubbed his brow. He had seen men look this way during and after the war, in particular those who had exited Andersonville. The poor bastards may have shown an emotional spurt at first, but in the end, they had grown detached. What in the world had this little girl witnessed to turn her this way?

A knock came at the door.

"That must be Doc Faraday," Emily exclaimed. "He'll know what to do."

The spectacled Fred Faraday made his way in, droopy-eyed and sluggish, his thick, white mane and mustache in disarray. "Sorry for the wait." He swung his bag about, looking for a spot to drop it. "Martha Peterson was my prior stop—moaning again about her aches and pains. It's all in her head, of course, but if I don't grant her attention, she'll harp that I don't give a hoot." He slid the bag onto Kendle's desk. "So, I hear you have a visitor in need of my services." His gaze fell upon the little girl. "Well, I'll be. There you are."

"Poor thing came to town screamin'," Kendle explained, "loud enough for the folks on the south side to hear. She's not speaking, though. Can't figure it. I caught a couple young fellahs passing by and asked them to fetch Emily before gettin' word to you. Assumed the child might be more at ease with a lady. Didn't work out so well."

Kendle's wife nudged him. "I did my best, Doc." She reached over and stroked the girl's curls. "The poor thing's in her own sad world."

Doc stepped before the child, thumbed her chin to inspect her eyes and then placed the back of his hand upon her forehead. "She's a tad warm, though it is a warm day." He bowed and smiled. "Don't feel like talking, eh? Can you at least muster your name, sweetie?"

The child remained mute.

Doc shook his head. "You know, there's been talk of the Dead Sheriff in these parts. Heard he made an appearance in Chesterfield. Killed a couple bandits. You from Chesterfield, honey?"

More mollified silence.

The doctor drummed his jaw. "Yeah, could be that Dead Sheriff, if he's as unsettling the majority claims. Of course, the legend does help the cause: all that more-or-less nonsense of how he wanted to protect his family...rose from the grave to exact revenge. Personally, I think it's just some damn fool in disguise. A friend of a friend says he saw the big galoot at a theatrical event in Kansas or Dallas or thereabout—sheer, sideshow fakery, I was told, even if the women did grow queasy upon seeing it...smelling it... whatever. Still, better the fright-face approach than what those niminy-piminy, masked vigilantes do. I'll tell you, I've heard some fishy things about that fancy-pants Silver Paladin and his snippy, little partner, Bullet, but I'll abstain from the details in the company of ladies."

Kendle grew impatient. "Come on, Doc. It's got to be more than a fellah in a disguise. I mean, look at her clothes."

Doc fingered the dried blood along the girl's sleeve. "I'll continue the examination."

The doctor proceeded to check the child and before long inferred, "Appears physically sound, outside of the stupefaction. The stupefaction is pretty acute, though."

Kendle shook his head. "Fine, Doc. How do we snap her out this, uh, stupefaction?"

"Rest is probably the best remedy."

Emily pulled her husband close. "We do have an extra bed. What would it hurt?"

Kendle shrugged. "It's fine by me, dear."

Doc grabbed his bag, and then he and the Kendle headed toward the door.

"I do appreciate you stopping by, Doc. I owe you."

"If Emily should make another of those blue-ribbon pies, please do keep me in mind."

Emily gave a playful wave. "Consider it done, Doc."

The men stepped into the warm, dusk air.

"Ah, before you go, Doc..."

"Yeah, Paul?"

"I didn't want to alarm my better half. She gets nervous about such things, but as you know, I've been concerned about certain activity within this vicinity."

Doc grumbled, fully aware of what he was to hear. "Go on."

"It's those, marauders. They're still roaming among the towns, coming and going at this point, but I'm sure planning to do more than steal. Often we can't figure who they are until after the fact, let alone what they're hoping to find, though they're likely checking for vulnerabilities. Now, I did alert the outside government to intervene with rangers and such, but as you know, nothin's come of it. Some say this vermin is growing in number. We shouldn't take such lightly. It's only a matter of time before something goes awry. Maybe it already has." He cocked his thumb back to the office. "I mean, that little gal could be a result."

Doc frowned. "We've discussed this before, Paul. You know how I feel."

"I'm aware of your position, and I know how the other council members feel. Listen, I respect the Quaker way of life, even if I'm not an official member of it. I believe it's best to be prepared. You don't like guns. I appreciate that, but if I'm the primary one here who's willing to shoot and kill, it's not going to help much. I don't even have an on-the-books deputy, Doc. At this point, we've gotta fortify this town. If there was anything I've learned from fighting Johnny Reb, it's never take anything for granted: that what happens to others won't happen to you. Now, that doesn't mean every man here has to be leapin' about shooting everything in sight. They just gotta be prepared."

Doc turned. "We'll bring it up at the next council meeting. I'll ask Mayor Pendrake to jot it on the agenda."

"You know, he'll sweep it under the rug. He's no better than Pastor Leigh. They never hear me out. But if you were to press the issue on them—to everyone in town—maybe then folks would take note."

"I'm sorry, Paul. Not much more I can do than I already have. If you want a town discussion, there's a process for it. I suggest you be satisfied with that."

Kendle turned, angry and frustrated. He looked to the forlorn sky, its clouds looking weird, like disjointed segments: an uneasy omen if ever there was one, he thought. Why the hell had he agreed to a job he could not perform to full capacity? Why did everything here have to be so judgmental, so puritanical?

As he watched Doc head away, he truly hoped the girl's condition was the result of some mad masquerader. If not, there was no telling what trouble lurked on the horizon.

CHAPTER NINE

Walsh trekked longer than intended. He could have hit at least one town by now, but the farther he traveled from Purity—from Perdifious—the more reckless he became.

What if he kept wandering, never planting the promised word? What would Perdifious care if his forlorn general abandoned the mission? Other men had left without apparent cause on occasion. As long as he did not taint his leader's image (do anything that might cause the fiend interference, let alone catch the man's mental stretch), that should suffice. Besides, Perdifous had a new right-hand man, did he not? If Perdifious preferred an unstable, ruddy sack of blubber in lieu of a loyal, clear-headed confidant, so be it. His friggin' loss.

Unfortunately, Walsh only had a pocketful of coins and in his zeal, had not thought to ask Perdifious for more. What he had was enough for a couple, conversational drinks before having to round up more to continue the crusade. To live, to expand beyond the horizon, no matter the intent, he needed funds.

With that notion planted, he headed farther beyond the beaten path. He had robbed more than a few folks in his travels and gotten a decent sum from the effort. Rich folks fancied adventuresome, scenic routes. In addition to money, they had jewelry and such.

He smirked at his cleverness. Yep, Pedifious was losing a smart one, all right.

A meandering pass appeared before him. He remembered covering it before: real nice and inviting. He pointed his horse toward it.

Now, it was just a matter of where to sneak and when to strike.

"It will be dusk soon," O'Malley warned. "Why not make camp, Sam?"

Sam glanced at the sky. He still didn't like the look of it, despite the twilight clarity. "I say we keep going."

"In the dark, on a trail we don't know?"

"Yes."

"Well, I must disagree. We should make camp, fix some dinner, get a good night's sleep and then make up the miles in the morn. Logical, don't you think?"

"To hell with logic."

"You have a contrary attitude, Sam. I don't know why you're acting this way."

Sam tugged the reins, halting the horses.

O"Malley threw up his arms. "Now, what? I was only trying to—"

"Someone's approaching."

Sam was right. O'Malley heard the clopping.

"Probably just a passerby," the Bostonian conjectured. "I say, who's there?"

No answer.

"Hush," Sam scolded. "I'll do the talking."

The hooves sounded more hurried. Then its rider, shadowed by a large tree came into view. He halted his horse, his gun catching a spurt of sunlight.

"Good gracious," O'Malley muttered.

Sam touched his gun. "I said I'll take care of it." He took a deep breath and calculated. "We don't want any trouble, mister. You let us pass. We'll let you do the same. Deal?"

"Sorry—no deal." Walsh led his horse a tad farther, the sunlight illuminating the bandit's unshaven scowl and scrawny frame. "I say, you hand over your goods, and then I'll be on my way. No one dead. Everyone happy."

"We've nothing to hand over."

Walsh shifted his eyes to O'Malley. "That fancy dresser says otherwise. Where'd you get that nice vest and cap? New York City?"

"Boston, actually," O'Malley corrected.

Sam groaned. "I said I'll handle this."

O'Malley sighed. "Sorry."

Walsh came closer. "Now, I'm going to dismount and head on over. You're going to take off that vest and cap, Mister Fancy Pants. Also, give me what's in your pockets. As for you, Injun, you're walkin' with me to the back of the wagon. Show me what you got in there. Hope that's not too complicated."

Sam half smiled. "Not at all." From the side of his mouth, he hissed to O'Malley, "Do what he says."

"Oh, for heaven's sake." O'Malley popped off his cap and slid off his vest. "I only have a few coins in my vest pocket. Nothing in my trousers."

Walsh leapt from his horse, patted it and approached with giddy grace. "I'll take whatever you got, no matter how big or small. I ain't fussy." He pointed his gun at O'Malley. "Just leave your things on the buckboard and that includes any pistols or knives you might have. You're then gonna stand next to that tree, your back to me. You budge in a way I don't like, and you're dead. Got that?"

"Yes, got it."

As O'Malley complied, Walsh swaggered toward Sam. "All right, Injun. You heard—no shenanigans. Now, hop down."

Sam leapt from the wagon and raised his hands.

Walsh gave him a shove and snickered. "Not that it matters, but where you boys headed, some posh get-together?"

Sam moved toward the rear. "A town called Purity."

Walsh paused. "Whoa, there. Purity you say?"

"Yeah, Purity."

"Well, what do you know? Hate to break this to you, but you're gonna be mighty disappointed."

"How's that?"

"Purity ain't no more. It's been seized by a madman and his gang: the worst of the worst in hopes of attracting more of the same. Not that I care, anymore. If you boys are lookin' to find religion, you'd be wise to stay clear of Purity."

The thief's claim surprised Sam. "Purity seized? How?"

"Not hard to figure, really, with the folks being unarmed and all gathered together as they were on a Sunday morn. Now, they're all dead—gunned down and I'd imagined, buried deep in the ground by this point. The almighty Palmer Perdifious orchestrated it. He's the mastermind."

A steely numbness overcame Sam, as Walsh gave him another shove.

"Unload your possessions, so I can inspect them in the light."

Anger seized Sam, his focus sharpening a hundredfold.

"Step to the side," Walsh commanded, peering into the opening. "Maybe I'll just see what's in there first."

As Walsh poked his head in, another surfaced, its face leathery under

"You're going to be mighty disappointed."

its big, smudged hat, eyes curled by sickly yellow—Colt raised.

"What the—"

The Dead Sheriff shot Walsh in the forehead, making his back snap as he struck the ground. A rush of gunsmoke swirled above his broken frame like a demented halo.

Sam's faithful zombie, yet propelled by his benefactor's lingering command, stepped out and stood with obedient rigidity, his odor wafting enough to spook the fallen man's mare, which neighed and galloped away in the opposite direction.

O'Malley dashed over. "Dear Lord. What's happened?" He regarded Walsh's body as the blood gushed from his brow, the man's glazed eyes twitching. "I suppose I shouldn't complain, but..."

Sam cupped the amulet, which felt warn against his skin. "I take it you heard what he said."

O'Malley nodded. "Could it be? I mean, the entire town?"

"Palmer Perdifious. That name familiar?"

"Not at all. Our friend said a madman and his gang had invaded. I suspect it's those raucous raiders we've heard about. Rumor has it they've been building in number, but they generally keep their distance on a whole."

"Maybe they've decided to branch out. That's all we need: a place where the worst elements converge. That's going to make it hard to catch anyone, let along collect bounties."

"Surely, Washington would intervene."

"The government should have done that already." Sam stretched. "We might as well head out, so we can verify things for ourselves."

"Yes, I do wish to validate that cretin's claim, but first, what do we do with the body?"

"Nothing."

"Pardon?"

"You said it's getting dark. Why waste time burying him? Let the bastard rot." Sam looked up. "If we keep a steady pace, we could make Purity by dawn."

"What if he has partners, friends who come upon his body and then track us down?" O"Malley looked about. "What if they're nearby, somewhere down the trail?"

"Then they'll catch up and bury him, and if they should cross our path, we'll tend to them just like we did him. Don't know why you're so worried. No one gets the upper hand on the Dead Sheriff and his trusty, Indian sidekick, Cheveyo. Read your own writings if you have any doubt."

O'Malley shook his head and walked away

Sam could not deny that O'Malley made some valid points. Even so, he felt it best to press on, albeit with caution. Who knew surprises Purity might bring? Ultimately, they would either click their heels in relief or face the dire truth. If the town was, in fact, ruled by the unruly, there was no telling how harsh things might play, even with the Dead Sheriff in tow.

CHAPTER TEN

The men spread like a great wave as Perdifious and the ersatz Crabby entered town, bowing and saluting.

Crabby had suggested that for the sake of effect, they go via wagon and located their best vessel (a veritable carriage or sumptuous stagecoach compared with the lackadaisical others) and latched it to two of their most winsome, black mares. He assured Perdifious that the ornamentation would enhance his ostentatious guise, and considering the men's awe-struck reactions, it succeeded in spades.

Crabby had also recommended occupying Wakefield's home and using it as their symbolic station, but Perdifious disagreed. For one, he did not fancy any one locale to dispatch orders and secondly, he had long shed the type of priggish décor that one like Wakefield would favor. (Hell, even the cosmopolitan women he preferred still required a seamy edge.) The church—that gesticulating hub of plundered hope—would be a more sensible springboard to administer his command.

As his luck would have it, the bodies (young, old, tall and tiny) had been hauled to the town's adjacent cusp, where a small cemetery had been erected by Wakefield's flock. His minions had shoveled it away, replacing it with an enormous, round pit into which the flock's fallen had been dumped. In the process, the workers had either uprooted or stomped the sparse markers that had been planted, each having conveyed nauseating slogans about fruits of labor and hard travel for the sake of some lofty goal. Pathetic.

Crabby removed an oil painting of the Last Supper from the rear wall of Wakefield's study, along with a cabinet that housed Bibles and theological texts. The desk was sturdier than the one he was accustomed to hauling, so that would stay, but not its dense cluster of matching chairs.

"I do believe," Crabby suggested, "that we should paint the chamber. Even if you only plan to use it temporarily, this drab white doesn't suit you. Black would be a far better hue."

"I prefer red, but the pigment will be remedied soon enough. For now, I must tend to another concern."

"As you wish, sir."

"Intuition tells me that Mister Walsh is through—not returning, that is. You will act as my new general, or is your devotion exclusive to the Master?"

"No, sir—yes, sir."

"Well, which is?"

"I serve both causes. To me, they're indivisible."

Perdifious eyed Crabby's cheeks. "You had a greenness about your complexion, subtle, but it was there. Now, it's a red, not too distinct, but more in line with your general look. Your shape—it's rounder, more hunched." Perdifious appeared pleased with his observations. "Your arms are longer, or is it your wrists and hands? Now that I think of it, when you took the reins, they did look all the more like claws." Perdifious rapped his fingers along the desktop and glanced about the chamber. "It appears I've gained a new, cozy throne, as well, but tell me my friend, at what cost?"

"Cost? There is no cost, unless you fail. You fail and you end up with nothing." Crabby clamped his fingers, accentuating his crustacean guise. "If I may be so bold, sir, you now reign over an entire town. Your men need not travel any longer, hide or creep throughout the night. That is, in its own devious right, a stupendous accomplishment."

"Perhaps, but how long will it last? Can you at least tell me that, my freakish friend? Will it all crumble after I have retrieved the amulet or before?"

Crabby considered the matter. "I would imagine either is a possibility, but only if you allow such. What you possess is the first step in an ascent to greatness. It's a matter of how you choose from here on. To maintain your status—your momentum—you would be wise to move fast. Besides, has it not been your desire to rule more than one sector, to eradicate all through a cascading path?"

The statement piqued Perdifious's interest. "Yes. Go on."

"Purity is but one town, an easy one for the taking, and as you've acknowledged, it will stand as a symbol of intimidation. You toss it away and seize another, your reputation grows even stronger. There are many other towns within this region: Chesterfield, Peach Water and Daisy Field. Perhaps for your next move, you should pick the most formidable, if only to make a point."

"None of them is formidable."

"Perhaps. However, the one you do pick matters for appearance sake.

Once you seize another town, you can more easily seize others. You will gather resources from each. From Purity, you have lumber, food, horses and wagons, if you do, indeed, want them. But from other towns, you could gain weapons. Even a small sum would prove beneficial. From there, you can add more and more to your arsenal. By the time any opposing force should come your way; you will be more than prepared. And, I might add, you also possess an advantage to rival any seasoned army."

"Advantage, you say?"

The demon tapped his temple. "Your virulent intuition. It will allow you to trap that avenging duo, or as it now stands, trio. I do believe you've harbored this plan of action in your subconscious. With Purity standing as a fallen symbol, a preordained magnet as it were, you have the chance to regain the amulet. This will please the Master, and the Master will not overlook the deed. He has immense influence. He can tarnish the land as well as you and therefore help spread the weeds of evil to solidify your reign. One dirty hand dirties the other, Mister Perdifious. That's the way quality pacts work."

Perdifious savored the prospect. "I see. So, I will suppress my trepidation to draw forth the trio, seize the amulet and then take my conquests to a higher level, with the Master's blessing."

"The sooner, the better, sir."

He closed his eyes and meditated. "The closest to Purity is Daisy Field. Might as well be Daisy Field. It has more edge than Purity, but still an easy enough notch in my belt to instill fear."

"Then Daisy Field it is. Your decision will fortify your cause. Your actions will send pulsations to ensure your success. Most good men will stay away, tremble at the thought of confronting you, but the Dead Sheriff and Cheveyo—that's the Indian's calling card, you know—will edge inward. So will their intrepid scribe. With their advent, you will have the chance to establish an irreversible, domino effect: an established catalyst for a veritable Hell on Earth, if you so wish it."

Perdifious grinned. "I do wish it, more than anything, but if you don't mind, I'm a sentimental sort when it comes to commemorative particulars. It seems only reasonable to christen this phase of my history."

He motioned his companion from the room, leading him past the pews. When they arrived at the row nearest the doors, Perdifious knelt and rubbed his palm into a puddle of congealing blood.

The two then stepped out and shut the doors, greeted by a euphoric rush of cheers and applause.

"No longer will this town be called Purity," he proclaimed to his mind-numbed admirers. He reached up, smearing across their white expanse, HA on the left, D overlapping them, ES to the right. "May this be the first of many."

"Yes, oh, yes," General MacIntosh concurred, his belly bouncing like contemptuous jelly. "Perfect, sir, perfect." His face turned a deeper red, his eyes black and beady. "Glory be—Hades, it is—the first of many."

CHAPTER ELEVEN

Sam directed the horses to Purity's farther outskirts, from where a distinct whiff of profane hollering and pistol blasts were heard.

"Doesn't sound very pure to me," O'Malley remarked. "Then again, my father often said, it's those self-proclaimed pious who are always the drunkest and foulest of mouth, given the chance. Perhaps this is some peculiar purgation ritual. I mean, it could be. I've heard that Wakefield's peers do consider his practices flagrantly optimistic."

Sam's agitation rose. "That's not the sound of a religious sect. It's got to be nearing dawn, and these coyotes are still carrying on."

O'Malley fidgeted and then asked, "Do you want to head in?"

Sam shrugged. "What's the point?"

"I know what we're hearing, Sam, but still to be certain on all counts, we need a viable vantage. What if Purity's people are being held captive? What if they need help? If so, we could send word in the very least, and if these pillagers are drunk out of their minds, they probably wouldn't notice us, anyway. We could stick to the shadows and blend in."

"We'd risk being moving targets."

"Maybe the Dead Sheriff could—"

"Don't entertain it. If I got him in, I'd have to get him out. That would prove tricky as hell. Let's wait till it's light." Sam leapt from the buckboard and yawned. "We'll rest a few hours. When things have hushed, we'll peek in. That's it."

O'Malley sighed. "As you wish my liege."

Sam headed to a cushy patch of grass, leaving O'Malley to gaze at the sky. Its starless blackness made the revelry all the more ominous.

He leaned back and tried not to let it bother him, thinking of the man the Dead Sheriff had killed earlier, how they had left his body unconcealed and wondered if the birds might have begun pecking at it. Such a horrid thought. How could he even hope to sleep?

He descended to the wagon and stroked the horses. He could tell the poor creatures were strained. That was Sam's fault, and there he was, curled up like a kitten, already snoring away.

O'Malley lit a cigar and decided to take a stroll and advanced a few safe yards at a time. However, as he got ever closer, he noticed flickering torches within, as well as men stumbling about. Drunk, all right.

With this, he got even bolder and crept farther, recalling how his father had often worked the night shift, moving through the dimness, scanning all corners, sniffing each crevasse, absorbing each incriminating detail. That's how the best sleuths did it.

The smell of flames and liquor grew stronger, luring him to the point of becoming hypnotized by the combined sensation. He kept going, his legs moving as if by some external force. He wondered if this was how the Sheriff felt when he was summoned.

O'Malley passed a queue of steeple-peaked homes. Pure as the driven snow, he thought. A bottle broke, more laughter followed, then another gun blast. There he was, all of a sudden right in the center of the sordid flow. He could not stop now, even if he wanted.

Men skidded by him, their clothing tattered, their eyes blurry. As he suspected, his presence mattered little, as long as he was careful. He then entered an area lit by gas lamps and further torches.

He heard giggling nearby, a kind of hiccupped gurgling. It came from a small man in a dusty suit, a slithery bow tie, dented Confederate cap (no doubt found or stolen) and grasping a bloodied knife as he tottered by. A short distance from him was a sprawled woman, her blue dress splattered in crisscrossing blood across her bosom, her bugged-eyed, severed head propped a few inches from her gushing neck. O'Malley cupped his mouth.

He then realized the craziness he had placed himself in and looked for a way out. How far had he wandered in? Each impetuous patch reminded him of a Hieronymus Bosch painting. Thank goodness he had his pistol strapped to him, though under these daunting conditions, he would need a lot more than that. At this point, would firing it prove effective or merely get him caught?

He heard more giggling—women this time, buzzing along the next street, at an alley's cusp. Several men prodded them, but the women's antics looked staged. (Did these women participate of their own accord or had they been forced into the frivolity?) One shrieked and flailed before being pulled from sight. Silence fell until more glass shattered, more guffaws and gunfire sprung, echoing off the facades.

He finished his cigar, tossed the butt and retraced his steps. Perhaps he could travel among the meandering paths to find release, but as he came to a dead end, he felt a presence behind him and turned.

The shadowy entity projected an abnormal roundness, and when the thing cleared it throat, it emitted an unearthly twinge.

O'Malley feigned a relaxed pose and tightened his knuckles. "Hello, there. Seems I've lost my way."

The figure swayed forward, grunting with arms outstretched.

"Now, keep your distance there, friend." O'Malley almost pulled his weapon, but decided instead to strike a pugilist pose. "I'm warning you. I'm trained in the arts."

The brute swayed faster and through naïve instinct, O'Malley charged full force into the obstruction. However, upon making impact, O'Malley bounced straight off his brute's belly and nearly lost his balance. Again, he raised his fists, but this time, his opponent leapt upon him, clamping O'Malley's shoulders with the gamut of his weight.

"Good Lord," O'Malley groaned, finding it impossible to breathe, let alone break free. His opponent then delivered a claw-like blow to his victim's brow.

O'Malley's consciousness faded. Crabby tossed him over his massive shoulder and with a coy, satisfied waddle, moved on.

CHAPTER TWELVE

O'Malley stirred within the gas-lit chamber, his vision blurred behind his glasses, his nostrils filled with the scent of blood. His head throbbed like a thousand hangovers, and his wrists were cuffed. The sides of each were welded to thick chains as he dangled from above. He discerned a desk, and below it, his short-brimmed hat, flattened and torn.

The feeling was far worse than when Damon and Emile Loizeaux, those detestable twins of evil, had strung him to a chair at the Dallas's Palisade Theater. At least he was not gagged this time.

"Where am I?" He tugged the chains, the weight of his boots making him twirl. "I say, where am I?"

"He does strike me as familiar." The voice was rich and robust. "However, when I envisioned him, he was distanced and of lesser significance than the corpse and Indian: merely one along for the ride, I surmised."

O'Malley felt another presence surface from the side. "I assure you," the entity stated with calm calculation, "he is precisely whom you suspect."

"Thank you for sniffing him out. I am in your debt, Mister MacIntosh." The icy sophisticate then prodded the top of O'Malley's head, causing him to flinch. "Ah, easy there, fellow. I only wish to inspect your wound."

O'Malley seethed, "I will ask again, and I trust you will tell me this time. Where am I?"

"You're in a chamber, hanging from a ceiling." The man's thick beard and a hint of his protruding scars filled O'Malley's view. "To be exact, you are in my place of work, formerly that of a renowned, pure-in-heart charlatan named Winifred Wakefield. My name is Palmer Perdifious. I now govern Purity, though have renamed it Hades. It only seemed right, considering the hellish aftermath my army administered." He touched O'Malley's crown again, but this time a tad harder. As O'Malley gritted his teeth and tears streamed, Perdifous snapped his wrist back, taking delight in O'Malley's ponderous twirl. "That's it, now. Very good. Jig those troubles away, my poor, manacled dandy."

O'Malley's heart pounded to the point of bursting. "You sadistic son of a—"

Perdifious placed his bloodied fingertip upon O'Malley's lips. "I'd think twice before expressing such disrespect, Mister O'Malley. Yes, I do know your name, and Mister O'Malley, you'd be wise to win my favor. You'll be hanging there for a good spell otherwise, but the choice is yours. I can set forth the torture with delicate precision—a tap here and there for a valuable word or two—or I can be sloppy about it, granting a fast torment the likes you've never experienced, in hopes of gaining it all. Either way, I get what I want."

Perdifious's companion stepped into the light, his insinuated features piercing O'Malley's haze, allowing him to recognize the brute even before the light cloaked him.

There was no doubt that he resembled a crab, but not in some slight, caricatured way. The resemblance was genuine, featuring a round, red mane and bright, clownish cheeks fringed by stark white skin. The entity's arms were clamped across his belly with two, large "fingers" that darted from out each clubby extension.

Perdifious turned to the crab-man. "Wouldn't you agree that the choice is his?"

"Entirely." The crab-man regarded O'Malley with pity. "As you say, sir, easy or hard. In other words, fast or slow, depending on his particular penchant."

O"Malley stiffened, thus ceasing his sway. "What do you want of me?"

"You already know the answer to that, Mister O'Malley. Again, it's your decision how this plays. I do take pleasure in inflicting pain, and if need be, death, each over the long haul and either one, you'll receive. Mister MacIntosh adheres to the same methodology. His purpose is to meet my criteria. With that said, for the sake of extending conversation, where might your faithful Indian companion be? Is he by chance wandering Hades's streets? What of the dreaded Dead Sheriff? Waiting in the wings maybe?" Perdifious pressed his cheek against O'Malley's and whispered. "I've no doubt your friends will come, drawn to your pain like a magnet to steel. That's the real reason I wish you to be tortured. I only give you the decorous option of how to magnetize."

O'Malley shook his head. "You work for the Master, You're one of his minions." He shifted his eyes to Crabby. "So's he."

Perdifious stepped back and sneered. "I work for no one but me, but since the Master has presented his proposal through a most convincing host, I've felt compelled to seize it. You fell right into my trap and sooner than I had hoped, pushing me closer to the amulet and that coveted chance to reap my rewards. A delicious deal, I dare say, and from what I can determine, fated."

Regret beset O'Malley. Why had he not listened to Sam and stayed put?

"The winds are blowing the symbolic flames, Mister O'Malley. My success is at hand. It's in the sky, the air. You can feel its poison curdling in the wind. Your pain will only marinate it."

He nudged his henchman. "Keep an eye on him, will you? I must meditate for a spell." He placed his bloodied finger upon O'Malley's chin and shoved him back. "I suggest you grant the same respect to Mister MacIntosh that you would grant me under these precarious conditions. Mr. MacIntosh has become, after all, a child of erratic rage."

The crab-man glanced to the left, where he had propped his axe, drawing O'Malley's gaze to it.

Perdifious reached the door. "I'll return shortly. Make certain that our prisoner is in a better mindset by such time."

"Will do," Crabby croaked, rubbing his claws.

As the door closed, O'Malley's consciousness crumbled.

So, he thought, this was how he would meet his end: like a chained animal set for the slaughter. A pity he could not document the grisly details in his journal. It would have been nice to convey his unjust fate, if only so that the world would know the monsters that sealed it.

Sam rolled about the grass; his slumber was raw and ambivalent.

At least morning would come soon. Then he and O'Malley would face the dreadful music, verify Purity's damage.

Things would never be the same. The impact of the town's assured destruction would stretch like wild weed. That's the way evil worked. One unjust event always pollinated another.

CHAPTER THIRTEEN

O'Malley heard Perdifious enter.

"I gave his weaponry to some passing buffoons," Crabby explained, "but thought it best to keep his spectacles on. In this way he might better appreciate the clarity of process. Granted, the lenses are a trifle splotched, but that couldn't be helped when tinkering with his head. The gash is much wider. He didn't budge much at all during the process. I even had to pinch him to make certain he was yet alive."

Perdifious regarded O'Malley's crimson face. "Be grateful that he is alive, Mister MacIntosh. Instinct dictates that we must maintain the proper pitch of panic for my technique to work effectively."

O'Malley cracked a languid lid.

Crabby waved his claw before him, pleased to see he had resumed cognition. "So, bodily vibrations are the charm?"

Perdifious snatched a small jar from the desk and with it, approached his captive. "Yes, they are." He turned just enough for O'Malley to see that the jar was empty, but its crinkled label conveyed an unsettling prospect: A skull with cross bones and the word, CYANIDE.

Perdifious removed the lid and held it beneath O'Malley's nose. "Please do take a whiff. The jar still harbors a distinct aroma."

The tartness made O'Malley's eyes water.

"Do you know why I keep this empty jar?"

O'Malley shook his head.

"I poisoned an entire orphanage—children and faculty—when I was thirteen, with the very contents of this jar. I poured it all into cake batter when the baker took a nap. From an article I later read, most of those infected died. Those few who did live, suffered for days on end and I'm assuming were shaken by the event for life. No one ever caught the culprit, but some did whisper his name." Perdifious beamed. "I used aliases for a time, but after enough travel, I discovered that few cared who had committed the crime. A shame, considering the magnitude of it, but I've never forgotten the satisfaction it bestowed. I have since yearned to rival it with a more heinous and enduring display."

He reattached the lid and regarded the jar with macabre reverence. "I believe I derived the ghastly idea to poison based on the whispers I heard behind the orphanage halls. My parents were said to have consumed poison tea to depart their lives. What better way to pay homage to them than by referencing the act? I knew it would be an ideal form of symbolic jest and one of great convenience since the poison had practically fallen into my hands. For symbolic purposes, I could have equally struck a match and burned the nauseating place down. Fire is a form of poison, after all, as I learned at a wee, tender age. For that matter, anything that changes a landscape acts the same way, with a deep, indelible scar marking that change." He fingered his cheek, parting his wiry strands to reveal the breadth of his purple curls. "And a scar, though ugly, need not be a detriment, but rather a badge of honor and a parabolic chance for many more such chances."

Perdifious rocked with pensive grace and slid the jar onto the desk, next to the flickering lamp. He then pulled from his coat pocket, a gleaming, hypodermic needle.

O'Malley quaked.

"It did not take long for me to become interested in various poisons and upon occasion, I tinkered with the ingredients I came upon. A doctor's medical bag—a reward from a random, road robbery—awarded me the initial chemicals with which to toy, along with this sterling device. It's been tested, I'll have you know, at first upon a lady we snatched along a dusty trail. I injected her several times over. She did not fare well, though the matter may have been due more to fear than the formula's spread. Perhaps I could have used it on her spouse instead, but Mister MacIntosh, while in his former form, clawed him dead after the fool had spewed some insults regarding our friend's facade."

Perdifious positioned the needle alongside O'Malley's cheek, allowing him to better appreciate its minatory construction. "On instinct, I experimented on myself, which proved hard, but after a number of doses and regurgitating symptoms, I came to formulate a potion that worked well enough for mind expansion. The result was painful but euphoric, and I noticed that with any self-inflicted wound—let's say a laceration on the thumb—the sting precipitated an echoing effect. This effect could extend in such a way that others might receive its vibrations. You'd be surprised how many of my subordinates would ask how I was feeling and with no cause to believe I was ill, beyond piqued intuition. I imagine my focus—my

"...the initial chemicals along with this sterling device."

mystical relegation—on the ingredients amplified the concoction to the point that we forged a basic mental exchange. I projected into the formula properties that mere chemicals could not induce. That method I still employ with any batch." He waved the needle like a wand. "I created my own anti-elixir, but there was never enough to pass along." His eyes glistened in line with the object's smearing sheen. "I was sure to store a batch for a special occasion like this. You are its honored recipient, Mister O'Malley. If by chance it should fail to achieve the desired result, well, there's always the axe."

"Please, no," O'Malley begged, his heart beating faster. "Please, there must be another way to resolve this."

Perdifious fingered the needle's point, positioned it at O'Malley's crown and sighed contently. He was enjoying this, O'Malley thought, as a piercing pain escalated, but after an unsteady moment, the madman removed the needle and glowered.

"Alas, this wound won't suffice." He aimed the needle at O'Malley's jugular and smirked. "Ah, yes, this spot will work much better."

O'Malley gurgled at the cold pinch and the subsequent flow, so smooth and warm.

"It's working, I do believe," Crabby commented with a cloddish clap. "I can see the fluid coursing."

"Indeed," Perdifious breathed. "The pulse of panic cascades like an enflamed gust. The pitch is perfect."

The room swirled before O'Malley's eyes, turning upside down and back again, shifting from left to right, right to left, its corners shrinking, expanding, as the lamp continued to beam in a steady ray through the jar, remaining on his brow, despite how he twitched.

"You cannot escape the poison's throes," Perdifious jeered, removing the needle and steadying O'Malley with a tight hand. "Your soul is one with the pain, the pain one with you."

O'Malley struggled, his body growing numb. He looked up, for he could no longer feel the clamps around his wrists. He was losing consciousness again, but this time a slither of his mind remained, funneling up and down and all around like a wily web.

Between his gossamer thoughts, the spectral town of Purity appeared, his mind scouring its paths, only then to leap beyond, skidding from town to city, city to town, river to sea, sea to river and at the hideous heart of it all, Perdifious's winged demons swirled, while a lime cloud broke and crashed. He saw children at a long table lined with cake, coughing; the crab-man (his features more subdued than now) swinging his axe, limbs severed and soaring, Perdifious looming in the forefront, a presiding shadow that had achieved its hateful fulfillment.

In O'Malley's head, Hell on Earth had become a reality, and with that terrifying realization, he bellowed from the pit of his frantic gut.

Perdifious sat in the pew from where he had scooped the christening blood, perceiving easy access to the rear and side entrances. The chosen vantage was but a pretext. It was the odious atmosphere he wished to suckle, the stench lulling him into a confident trance.

He realized that he was in a place from which all future carnage would stem. From henceforth, no one would dismiss his monstrous acts. The name Palmer Perdifious would be carved in infamy. Those he once feared, the Dead Sheriff and Cheveyo, could only ensure it.

CHAPTER FOURTEEN

Sam sprung up, his face scorched from the sun, his chest—and amulet—wet with sweat. He thought he heard something, felt something. What the hell was it? The remnant of an anguished dream?

He glanced at the wagon and wondered how much time had lapsed. Surely by now, O'Malley would have made breakfast or in the least, would be milling about.

Sam headed toward the horses and rubbed his eyes.

"O'Malley, I do believe we're tardy." Through the hazy, mid-morn light, he peered at the town's outer rim. "Maybe we should skip the inspection."

He looked inside the wagon, at the casket.

"O'Malley, where the hell are you?"

Goddamn, impatient fool. Had he ventured forth on his own?

Sam climbed the buckboard and steered the horses toward the town, rolling along its perimeter, but as he traveled, a disturbing bellow stalked him. Was it real or imagined? For the life of him, he could not tell.

The sky darkened. Thunder clapped. Rain fell and thickened, making it hard to see.

He circled faster, coming upon a large stretch of dirt, an evident pit that had been filled, but for what purpose? He glanced to the side and saw trampled crosses.

Through the wagon, he felt a curious vibration and within an instant and without apparent cause, envisioned its writhing souls, anchored by an injustice that made his skin crawl.

He then saw an elderly man dressed in black, looking upon him with apparent concern.

The man tipped his wide-brimmed hat, revealing the bluish hole of his brow, his translucent frame wavering within the drilling rain. He pointed yonder to a lonesome, white church.

Sam's curiosity piqued. "Who are you?"

The specter smiled.

Sam's intuition rose. Somehow, someway, he knew the man's name. "You're Winifred Wakefield."

The specter nodded, his smile fading.

"What's—what's happened here?"

The pastor lowered his head, the rain dashing through his form like tears.

"Please, sir—tell me."

Wakefield looked up, as if directing a rage toward God.

"They stole it from us," he replied, his voice twirling about Sam's head, "along with our lives. Palmer Pedifious—he's the one who ordered it. He's the one who inspired his men to slaughter us in our church. I can't say how I know this, but I do. I've prayed for answers, for any reason to explain the terrible event and received his name over and over again like the beating of a drum—a mockery to the sanctity of our Lord, if the Lord even exists." He spread his arms and glared with defiance at the stormy rage. "Why would the Father leave us to such torment?" He shot Sam a desperate glance. "Why? Please tell me, Cheveyo, is there any chance we might be avenged, any way we might be set free?"

The inquiry startled Sam, not to mention hearing his alternate name.

"I don't know, Pastor. I only heard someone moaning. I think he might be my friend." Sam regarded the church, and in reply, another coarse cry arrived. Sam turned back to the specter, but without warning, Wakefield was gone, his imprint washed away by the elements.

The cries heightened, and Sam felt the pricking impact of O'Malley's pain. There was no time to waste. He had to get inside the church: a risky prospect for certain, but he did have at least one formidable advantage.

As the rain whipped against the wagon, Sam guided the horses over the graveyard and stopped toward the church's rear. His focus—his command—increased. He slid off the buckboard and met the Sheriff halfway, giving the corpse the lead. The Sheriff ascended the platform and with a determined thud, pounded the door from its hinges.

Sam heard nervous shuffling within, followed by more moaning. He directed the Sheriff toward an adjacent chamber.

However, no sooner had they reached its threshold, Sam froze. He saw O'Malley dangling from the ceiling, his face a pulverized mess, large patches of blood decorating the rear wall.

As a perturbing light swirled within, a hunkered entity appeared, swaying near the desk, upon which an ominous lamp, jar and hypodermic needle sat. The thing's black, beady eyes protruded; its hair and skin red, with melded fingers and knobby, truncated thumbs.

Sam motioned the Sheriff onward, the corpse's arms raised to break O'Malley chains, but the crab creature bounced to the side and clamped its axe.

What transpired then was rapid and fierce, with the crimson monstrosity swinging with wild abandon, but Sam's agility kept the Sheriff fluid, so that for a time, the cadaver eschewed the crab-man's clunky advance.

This was, of course, not the first axed assailant Sam and the Sheriff had faced. In fact, the Sheriff had temporarily lost his left arm due to his melee with a brain-battered bootlegger called Stride, but as bad as the altercation was, it was against a mere man and this individual was (to say the least) something more or less than that.

Sam gestured the Sheriff to grab his Colt, but as the corpse began to pull the trigger, the crab-man cut before the desk and knocked it from his hand, its bulky blade slicing through the Sheriff's palm and into his wrist.

It was the same arm the Sheriff had "mended." The prospect of a repeat vexed Sam. At the same time, he dismissed the prior axe battle as a mere practice run. No matter how formidable this new competitor, Sam knew what to do and angled the Sheriff in hopes of averting full severance.

With a tight, dry fist, the Sheriff clobbered the creature's crown, making it fall to its knees, even though the blade tore farther into his wrist.

As if spurred by some inner will, the Sheriff shook the blade from his leathery skin, causing a cloud of blue bile to splash across his opponent's face.

The creature sneezed and attempted to rise, but the Sheriff pounded upon the thing's neck with uncompromising vigor.

Sam watched the shell-like coating around the crab-man's neck blister and crack and then guided the Sheriff to apply greater pressure onto the area until the crusty layer caved.

"Harder," Sam insisted, extending his arm, cranking his fingers. "Harder."

The crab-man's throat exploded, blood spurting high. A greenish goo followed, turning misty and ascending toward the ceiling. The creature emitted a death rattle, conveying its inexorable demise.

Sam cocked his arm back, thus softening the Sheriff's grip, while a green gush dripped down his tattered sleeve, only to evaporate into its threads. The crab-man's head wobbled to the side, black eyes turning gray.

Sam snatched the Colt, shoved it into the Sheriff's holster and with an anxious jerk, inspected the split limb.

It looked bad, but it would no doubt heal. He then grabbed the Sheriff's other arm and directed him toward O'Malley's chains. The Sheriff's fingers tightened and tugged until their friend fell free.

Perdifious's brain danced with the drumming, windswept rain, the noise nostalgic, but it was broken by a discordant shuffle.

From off the pew, he peeled himself and ran to his torture chamber, anxious to discern the cause.

"Mister MacIntosh—what's happened?"

He peered into the chamber, spotting MacIntosh's crushed body on the floor, blood still flowing from his neck. A tall, brooding shape stood nearby, O'Malley's jellied frame propped against the wall, chains snapped, cuffs unhinged.

Perdifious shook with rage as he watched the Indian move forward, his fist poised to punch, but instead of Sam delivering the blow; it was the Sheriff who punched Perdifious's face.

The villain's eyes rolled upward, allowing the Sheriff to strike again, this time far harder, causing the mad mystic to hit the floor.

For a moment, Sam came close to shooting him. An intuitive whisper told him this man was the ringleader. Sam could see it in his scars, in the sinister shape of his beard, but then decided, "Got to keep quiet. Got to get the hell out of here."

The Sheriff flung O'Malley over his shoulder, an awkward maneuver considering that he had but one viable arm. Nevertheless, he managed the task and shuffled out of the church, back into the rain and toward the wagon.

The Sheriff dropped O'Malley into the casket, and from there, Sam covered his friend with blankets. He grazed O'Malley's cheek and checked his pulse. Thank God, he was still alive.

"I'll get help," Sam told him. "Hang on, O'Malley. Please, hang on."

Sam directed the Sheriff to sit upon O'Malley's trunk, leaving the corpse's shoulders to fall back upon the wagon wall.

"Don't fret, compadre. You'll get your bed back soon enough."

Sam hopped out of the wagon, bolted to the buckboard and prompted the horses ahead. Within the arduous storm, they became a blurred fixture.

After covering about a mile, the wind and rain ceased. The sun returned, its blaze warm and assuring, but as welcome as it was, it did not quell Sam's trepidation.

He assumed that the Master had likely dispersed these new henchmen in advance, knowing somehow or other the three would arrive. If but for the luck of the draw, Sam may have been captured, as well, the amulet seized.

Though he was grateful for the fortunate turn, this was no time to rejoice. He had to get O'Malley to Daisy Field. It was their only chance, their only hope.

CHAPTER FIFTEEN

Cindy sat mute on a frilly bed in an oversized dress that Mrs. Kendle had borrowed from one of the neighbors. Books, more aimed at adults than children, were spread before her; supper almost ready. Though Cindy appreciated the lady's coddling, the girl's maddening melancholia lingered and with it, her rage.

She grew weary of the flanking contrivances and walked to the window to stare into the dusk-draped town.

Though she could not see it, she sensed the wagon rolling forth, its hooves inundating her ears.

She smiled. Before long, justice would come.

To push the horses further would have been futile and cruel. Sam was thankful, therefore, when he spotted the daisies.

He stopped at the town's cusp, hopped down and entered the rear. He patted O'Malley's face, checked his breathing. To avoid unnecessary questions and to keep the Dead Sheriff concealed, he had to carry O'Malley into town.

The Sheriff's bad arm had begun to reconstruct: bile and soot congealing it. The Sheriff could return to his coffin, undetected, unless someone dared to inspect.

Grunting and heaving from O'Malley's heft, Sam waddled across the fringing vegetation and entered the town.

The expanse looked desolate and so he hollered, "Anybody here? Please—anybody?"

A balding, middle-aged Negro appeared from out a small, blacksmith shop, apron dangling as he tucked a rag into his back pocket.

"Say, what's wrong, Mister?

Sam swung round to reveal his flaccid friend. "We need a doctor."

The blacksmith winced and pointed yonder. "Doc Faraday's right down the road. I can walk you there."

"Much obliged, sir. Much obliged, indeed."

The man took the lead. "So, what happened?"

"My friend got the tar knocked out of him and who knows what else. May have been poisoned, injected with somethin'. Trust me, it's complicated."

The blacksmith picked up pace as a white house came into view, potted daisies adorning its spacious porch.

"Here we are—Doc's place." The man skipped onto the porch. "He hits the sack early, but he'll help." The man knocked with urgency. "Doc's good that way."

After an interminable stretch, a gray-haired woman in a robe greeted them. "Why, Mister Elroy, what can I do for you?" She noticed Sam and O'Malley. "Oh, my."

"Sorry to trouble you, Cassandra, but as you can see, these men need assistance. One was beaten, poisoned perhaps. Hoping Doc'll look him over."

A gaseous glow flickered within. "I'm comin'. I'm coming'," a gruff voice called. "Give me a chance now, will yah?"

The old woman pouted. "Fred's had a tough day. For one, it's that Peterson woman, you know, always nagging about her aches and pains, and then of course, that little girl. So strange."

Doc hobbled to the threshold, his robe skewed, his hair twisted like a petulant pixie's. He adjusted his spectacles and looked past Elroy and scrutinized the men.

"My friend's in bad shape," Sam grunted, twisting around, so O'Malley became more visible. "Got roughed up, as you can see. Don't know how much longer he'll hold on."

The doctor stepped onto the porch and raised O'Malley's head. "What in the world?"

"He had a clash with some bad men. Please, we've traveled a long way. Can you help?"

Doc looked to Elroy. "Lead 'em round back." He then said to Sam, "I promise I'll do my best."

They headed around the side, into the doctor's office, a humble, but well equipped space toward the rear of the house, and placed O'Malley on a medical table.

"Where you from stranger?" Doc asked.

"Just about everywhere. Name's Sam. My friend is Richard O'Malley. He's a reporter from Boston—the Boston Globe, to be precise."

"I see. Well, I'm Fred Faraday. Folks generally call me Doc. My wife's Cassandra, Cassie for short." Doc spread O'Malley's hair. "That's a nasty wound. I need to clean him off, cool him down. Cassie, would you be so kind to get me a cloth and some water?"

As his wife exited, Doc frowned. "Where did this altercation happen?"

"Purity."

Doc winced. "Purity?"

"That's right. The town's under siege. We heard lots of revelry from the perimeter. O'Malley ventured in to inspect when I was sleeping. I knew something was wrong when I couldn't find him and then snuck in. Found him in that condition, chained to a ceiling in the back room of their church."

The doctor and blacksmith exchanged uneasy glances.

Cassie handed Doc the cloth and a pail. Doc removed O'Malley's glasses and wiped away the caked blood.

"I can stitch him up, but that won't be enough to make him right." He pointed at O'Malley's neck. "Looks like he was pricked by a needle—deep, too. Real sadistic." He checked O'Malley's eyes. "He's got something in his system, all right. No doubt of that."

Sam grimaced. "You have an antidote?"

"Antidote? I wouldn't know where to begin, son. Best I can do is patch him up, get him to the guest room, and then we pray for a positive outcome. If you want, you can occupy the room and keep an eye on him."

Sam appreciated the offer, but he could not leave the Sheriff unattended. "If you don't mind, I'd prefer to stay in my wagon. I'd just get edgy if I had to watch my partner suffer like this."

The doctor shook his head. "As you wish. How about giving Elroy a hand then? The guest room's upstairs."

Sam grabbed O'Malley from under his arms and Elroy grabbed his ankles. The doctor led them to a room at the end of the upstairs hall, where he instructed them to place O'Malley on a frilly bed. The doctor stripped O'Malley down, slipped him into a night shirt and then called down to his wife to stock the bed table with the basic necessities. From there, Doc and Elroy returned downstairs and waited on the porch, while Sam got his wagon.

He steered his vessel alongside the porch and for a spell just listened to the men whisper about the situation's dynamics, agreeing their sheriff should be informed. Soon thereafter, Elroy dashed off.

So be it, thought Sam. He could handle a lousy interrogation, but poor O'Malley probably would not recover, and that was not the worst of it.

For all intents and purposes the Master now possessed an entire town of ripe minions. Daisy Field would be their nearest attraction, and for that tragic turn, Sam cursed himself.

CHAPTER SIXTEEN

Perdifious squirmed about the floor, bent by shame, glaring at the snapped chains and cuffs, the green-smoked ceiling and of course, his henchman's flatulent shell. It had reverted to its flabby, human guise, the axe alongside it: a mocking symbol of futility.

Oh, what maddening mortification! He had both the Sheriff and Cheveyo right in his grasp, along with the perfect battered bait. He let all three flee—with the amulet, no less. If only there was a way to reverse the process, restage the variables to his favor.

A cold, pressing wind rushed in. The room darkened.

"My agent gave you instructions," a sinister whisper conveyed, "and yet you have failed—and now do no more than rest and wait. Why, Palmer Perdifious? Do you anticipate the demons of your mind to take up the reins for you?"

Perdifious sat up and looked about.

"Again I ask, for what do you wait? Why not let your rage dictate the terms. Rage eclipses misdirection and spreads like the poisonous weed you know too well."

"I'll track them," Perdifious committed with vehemence. "I'll track them and—"

Through Perdifious's blurry view, he saw the Master's blurry shape hovering above the desk like a crafty, carney projection, while a nondescript, green entity cut into the scene in hazy overlap. Perdifious realized the two stemmed from distant locales and sensed their physical attributes may have been abetted by his imagination as much as any accuracy.

"Track them, you shall, Perdifious—and when you do, you will gain another step toward what you desire. The next victory will be of a higher caliber and therefore, one of greater meaning. As my acolyte implied, let Purity stand as your practice run, an ambitious folly to initiate a long line of conquering scars."

The lamp's tempting glow filtered through the jar and into Perdifious' eyes.

"The symbol beckons," the Master hissed. "It reinforces who and what you are. Resign your overconfidence. There will be more than enough time for such triviality after the poison spreads."

In a calamitous swoosh, the Master vanished, followed by the green cloud, but a remnant of wind still whistled within, strong enough to topple the jar from the desk.

Perdifious sprung for it, but all too late, for it shattered upon the floor, its shards bouncing against Crabby's mountainous frame, its detached, crossbones label curling like a enflamed leaf.

The wind subsided, and Perdifious cringed over having lost this sentimental symbol of his past.

But the past was the past. A mere poisoning could not match the conquests he desired, and Purity a mere trickle to mark all that was to come.

The Dead Sheriff and his pawns may have fled. So be it. That they had crossed paths was but the first step: a taunting instigator that only made Perdifious ever angrier, ever hungrier.

"Glad you caught me before I closed shop," Kendle remarked, as he walked next to Elroy.

"If you weren't hanging around that damn, useless jail," Elroy replied, "your home would have been my next stop. I'm serious, Paul. This couldn't wait."

"So, this man, this, uh, reporter fellah, is in real bad shape, you say."

"Yeah, battered up in an awful way. Unconscious. The Indian told us what happened. I do believe his account's sincere."

"Well, I warned folks about those goddamn raiders. I told Doc it was only a matter of time before they started picking off innocent folks, but he's got to go along with those council jackasses."

"I'll say this much. Doc did look riled, real concerned. Maybe he's having a change of heart, especially with that little girl figuring in, as well. You know, it might not be a bad time to show him our stockpile. If he sees it, he might realize how serious we are about fortifying the town. He might be more willing then to convince the others."

"Ah, what's the use, Elroy? It's probably a lost cause. Even if Doc did manage the gumption, would it be enough to tip the scale? People can't be told what to do. They have to want to pick up arms and fight. They've got to have the heart for it. That's the way it works."

As they approached the porch, Doc greeted them, leaning against the side post, speaking to Sam, who was still on his wagon, looking drained yet edgy.

"So, you don't know if the entirety of Purity was occupied," Doc stated. "If you only entered the church, how could you?"

"Listen to me," Sam explained. "It adds up. First off, a man tried to rob us along the way. When he learned we were headed to Purity, he enlightened us on the situation—shoved our faces in it, in a way. We were cautious when we got to the town and held our ground outside it when we heard the ruckus: not the type religious folks make by any stretch. I also came upon a burial ground before I headed in for my partner. The dirt was fresh, and I could feel—" Sam caught himself. "Let's just say, it didn't feel right, didn't look right. I got good instincts when it comes to that sort of thing, having Indian blood and all."

Kendle and Elroy approached the steps and acknowledged the men with a brief, obligatory exchange. Doc then excused himself to Sam, and the three headed in.

Once O'Malley's condition was confirmed, the trio returned outside.

"You said he was captured." Kendle gave Sam a hard look. "You broke him free, got him out. Doesn't sound like an easy task."

"It wasn't." Sam did not wish to rehash the details. "I fought two of them. We were lucky to have escaped."

"And you visited Purity for what reason?"

"It was the next town up." He hesitated. "I'm a bounty hunter. My

"You broke him free, got him out."

friend's a writer. He's been documenting my exploits. Anyway, I comb the towns for wanted postings and various leads. That's all. Why would Purity be any different, even with its church-going angle?"

Kendle ruminated the matter. "Do you think those bastards might track you?"

Sam frowned in shame. "You're not safe, if that's what you mean, but I do believe these characters would arrive whether I was here or not. They have one town. They'll want another. Still, as for the timeline, I can only speculate, but usually these sadistic types move fast once they get a notion in their heads. I say it's best you get armed and ready as soon as possible."

Kendle ticked his tongue. "This is a religious town, just like Purity, with a lot more faith in the Lord than pullin' the trigger."

"If that's the case, then you got a huge problem on your hands. I left one of O'Malley's captors dead, the other unconscious, but when he wakes, I've no doubt he'll want to get even. I could leave and I probably should, but again, that won't make much difference. If these men come—and I dare say, they will—they'll want more than just me. They'll want to do to Daisy Field what they did to Purity."

Doc glowered at Sam. "Damn it all."

"I'm sorry. Truly I am. I acted on impulse. I needed to save my friend. That's all I cared about."

"You didn't do anything wrong," Kendle said with a compassionate sigh and then looked to Doc. "I told you. I warned you about this."

Doc bristled. "Well, we could dispatch some men in the morn. They could check on Purity to be certain—"

"Hell, Doc. There you go again, prolonging the inevitable. We've known about these men for how damn long now? We know Purity to be pious to a fault and therefore open to danger. We ain't much better. You want the same outcome for us?"

Cassandra stepped onto the porch.

Kendle pointed to her. "You want to put your wife in jeopardy? You want people killed? You saw that little girl. She can't even talk. She saw something—something I suspect that only real bad men could have done."

"You're making assumptions," Doc argued. "You're—"

"You're a goddamn fool, Doc. For Christ's sake, it's obvious. For all your learnin', I'd think you'd have more sense." He looked at Sam. "I believe this man. I believe we've great reason to be concerned."

Cassandra cleared her throat, catching Doc's attention. "Maybe he's right, Fred. Maybe we should be prepared, just in case."

Doc tugged his ear and grumbled. "All right, I'll touch base with the council first thing in the morning. I'll go straight to the mayor to schedule an emergency meeting. We'll go from there."

"And the meeting can't be a week from now, Doc," Kendle insisted. "We can't risk any dilly dallying."

"All right, Paul, all right, and I suppose it'll fall on me to persuade these folks to see it your way. I'll try, but I only wish I had the influence. Besides, beyond the few guns you got at the jail and some shared hunting rifles, what do we have to fend off any potential invaders?"

Elroy pulled Kendle near and whispered in his ear.

Doc waddled toward them "You fellows got something to say?"

Kendle shrugged, figuring he might as well divulge their secret. "We've been stockpiling weapons. They're stored in that tool shed I made, the one behind my house."

Doc raised an eyebrow "And may I ask, how much do you have at your disposal?"

"A lot, Doc. We might as well show it to you. Seein' is believing', after all."

Doc raised his hands. "Not tonight. I'm pure tuckered out from surprises. Best I'll do is visit at dawn, before going to the mayor."

"Fair enough." Kendle turned and motioned Elroy to follow, but as they departed, Sam called, "If you don't mind, I'd like to see that arsenal."

Kendle turned, surprised by the request. "I appreciate the offer, but I don't see—"

"That's right, you don't see. You don't see how I can be to your advantage, but I know more than a thing or two about firearms."

"So do I, son. I fought in the war—a Union lieutenant, I'm proud to say. There ain't nothing you can tell me that I don't already know."

"But I have a firsthand account to share. It might help to convince your people to pick up arms. I only ask in return that I help with the cause, that I have the chance to see what you have."

Elroy nudged the sheriff. "Why not? I mean, if he's willing to speak..."

Kendle groaned. "All right, you can see what we have. Doc will show you the way—break of dawn—and then he'll set the rest in motion. I want that meeting no later than tomorrow night. You hear that, Doc?"

Doc nodded and watched as the men marched off. He then turned to Sam. "You get your rest, son, but I'm telling you, the house would be warmer than that wagon."

"He's right," his Cassandra added. "It is getting a trifle chilly."

Purity

81

Sam appreciated the offer, but did not budge, not with the Dead Sheriff in his possession. "Again, I'll be fine as it is. Thank you, though."

Doc pointed toward the back of the house. "I have a small barn, or to be more precise, an oversized shack, where I keep some odds and ends. It's a few yards from Cassie's garden. Why don't you pull your wagon in there? It'll at least keep you from the elements."

Sam glanced at the murky, red-shingled structure.

"Thank you. I do appreciate it. That goes for you, too, Mrs. Faraday."

"You're welcome," she replied, "and if you should need anything, something to eat or whatever, I'd be happy to oblige."

Sam smiled. "Right now, shuteye is all I need."

"Don't we all?" Doc added.

Sam winked, tugged the reins and led the horses toward the structure. Yeah, he needed sleep, but could he really attain it?

The "barn" was spacious, dry and cool with a few wall shelves that held Doc's old medical bags, beakers, shovels and rakes. Once he felt settled, Sam shut the doors and motioned the Dead Sheriff to sit up.

"Now, let's see." Sam straightened the corpse's hat and with some spit rubbed a little gleam into his badge. He could not deny that he held a fondness for this particular model. They had been through a lot together, enough that it bothered him to think his compatriot could one day be damaged beyond repair. How many times would the healing properties recur before ceasing? The poor bastard had even survived a barrage of Gatling-gun fire. That had to have taken a significant toll, if not on the outside, then surely within. On the other hand, the Sheriff did seem to reform each and every time and much quicker than in the past.

He also showed more frequent signs of autonomy. He had even insinuated such when combatting the axe-wielding crab-man. Sam was not yet inclined to call it a genuine memory pattern by any means, but he could not help but suspect the corpse was learning a little here and there, to some extent or another.

"Glad the ol' arm didn't get chopped off, partner. You see, we learn from our mistakes. It all comes down to experience. No magical manual required." He made the Sheriff raise his arm. "Mending real fine, though your shirt's a mess." He tore off a sliver of sleeve. "I'll get you another down the line, something in brown or red instead of that stain-prone gray.

You'll look real dapper, while still scaring the shit outta folks. How's that strike you, partner? A nice, two-fold effect."

The corpse's jellied yolks beamed ahead, and though Sam had not expected an answer, he thought it might have been nice.

"Are we good men or bad, Sheriff? You tell me."

No reply was required. The Sheriff was, in fact, an instrument that dealt bad to gain good. If bad had any part in his actions it swung right back to Sam. Doing bad was nothing to be proud of, Sam knew. If anything, it made him no different than those he tracked, not to mention those who tracked him, or so one could philosophize.

"We do what we can, right, Sheriff? Hope for the best and all that."

He prompted the Sheriff to recline into the crate and slid the canvas covering over it. He then selected a hardy hunk of frayed hay to curl upon and closed his eyes. Slumber came only after an arduous spell, and even then it did not last long, for a violent vibration insisted that he rise.

The Silent Ones had arrived. Sam had anticipated this strange group of seven; or at least some such related phenomena of cryptic disposition. It was just the way things streamed these days since he had become a beacon to apparitions.

In truth, to label the Silent Ones as apparitions felt inaccurate. They were more like cultivated visitors from some celestial plane, their hooded, thin-lipped countenances obscured (and therefore made ever more regal) by a wild, crisscrossing, gray light that buffered behind them like a large, organic curtain. Sam sensed urgency within the anomaly and presumed it matched their mindset.

With much anticipation, he spun upon the hay and was about utter a jeering hello, but no sooner had his lips parted, a spark of light, brighter than that of the crackling gray, formed before him, eclipsing the entities.

It was Old Luke, his beloved, long-ago mentor from New Mexico. At least it appeared to be Luke. There was no real telling when his semblance manifested. For all Sam knew, the outlined image may have been a ploy prompted by the seven, but whatever the connection was, he was not inclined to unravel it.

Luke fanned his piano-player fingers and hunched his way forward, while his tangled beard, derby and checkered vest gained color.

Sam crossed his legs, dousing his doubts. Whether real or fabricated, it was sure nice to see his old friend again. He owed the man much for sharing the basics of life, including a tidbit or two here and there about the occult.

"I'm all ears, Luke."

"I'm sure you are and dang anxious for me to spill the beans, but this is a tough one, Sam, more entangled than you're accustomed to. The entire vicinity's gone sour. That sort of thing'll happen when blood runs thick. It gets like poison, you know. Some claim the same phenomenon was identified by the more astute during our civil rift, though any war has been known to trigger the pigmentation. Once it starts, you just don't see it. You taste it: doom and gloom layered upon layer, heavier than the heaviest soup."

"So, there's no doubt of it then. Trouble's coming."

"Yep, and that's puttin' it mildly."

"How much time have we?"

"Shit, not much. I really don't know how you and the Dead Sheriff are gonna handle it, let alone these nicety-nice Quakers. They're way stubborn in their passive principles, but I do believe they'd budge once guns were pointed at 'em. It's more a matter of how skilled they are when the onslaught strikes. They gotta be whipped into shape, first by gettin' their heads screwed on straight and then with some serious, firearm practice. If only there was more time..."

"What do you suggest?"

Luke shrugged. "How should I know? Battles—wars—they're tricky things, Sam. Lot of it comes down to the luck of the damn draw, who's positioned here or there when the bullets soar and I dare say, who wants it more."

The background snapped like a wave of chains, the effect so alarming as to make Sam wonder if he should dash away from it all, but of course, he was too conscientious to do that.

"I know this much," Luke continued, his squinty eyes weighed with burden. "If this thing tips in your favor—the favor of Daisy Field, that is—all will clear up fairly fast. Right now, there's lots of spiritual activity brewin'. Wakefield is behind a large chunk of it, though it's not his fault entirely. He's hankering for justice and so are his people. They know who put them where they are. That anger keeps them from moving on. While they linger, the air's gonna stay awfully strange. It's gonna push things this way and that. Maybe it'll make the situation better. Maybe it'll make it worse. No matter how it's tossed, the atmosphere's gonna be real, damn ugly for a decent while and so's everybody within it, alive or dead."

"Doesn't sound very encouraging."

"It ain't, but it's best you know what you're up against. This atmosphere—

this twisting and turning of the winds, if you will—it can do things to a man's mind. That's never good if the man in question has a task to fulfill. You've learned to operate the Dead Sheriff pretty well, but that operation could skip a beat, get bogged down by distractions. To rephrase, you might get confused. Just expect the unexpected, I say. Let your mind flow from there."

Sam groaned.

"Oh, and don't think any of this will be blown over in its final moments by the demonized wind. This won't be a Damnation purge, in other words. I'll give you that. And it won't be like fighting fanged whores, smelly cannibals or sick-to-the-core French Canadian twins. Cripes, you don't even have Hattie Fields to go along for the ride, which let's face it, would be an awful big advantage to the cause. As it therefore stands, Perdifious's hateful ambition has done a thorough job cloudin' the scenery. This villain prefers cutthroat challenges and to-the-death duels, even more than he does the arcane arts. He hopes to terminate every speck of peace and virtue along the way. In other words, the dirt and grime comprise the asshole's armor. His style is scratched deep into the fabric of this current reality, enough to devour any competing force, magical or otherwise. That's not to say you and the Dead Sheriff can't hold your own, but the circumstances will be more demoralizin' than you might wish to know."

"Wonderful. The prospect warms my heart."

"Yeah, I know it's a heap to stack on your shoulders, Sam, but you'll do what's necessary, even with the limitations." Luke gave a blurry bow. "Best of luck. You're sure as hell gonna need it."

Sam sighed.

Luke crackled away into pinpricked smoke, as did the Silent Ones and their amorphous backdrop.

Damn it, thought Sam. The situation seemed doomed. Why try to fix it? And yet to resign, to cower would be nothing short of sinful.

He had to stay strong, and if he stayed strong, so would the Dead Sheriff. Through his resurrected counterpart, maybe, just maybe, a solution would be had. If not, he would still do everything in his power to remedy the dilemma before Heaven or Hell dared dictate the terms.

CHAPTER SEVENTEEN

Sam woke to a rooster's crow and hobbled off the hay, grateful for, but still troubled by, Luke's perplexing proclamation. He would keep his trepidation tucked behind a frigid facade. An expression of doubt could prove contagious.

He opened the barn doors. Doc was standing there, dressed in suspenders and thin, black tie, about to knock. He cracked a grin.

"Cassie made breakfast. I suggest you take her up on it. Paul can wait a spell." Doc turned. "Your friend's holding his own, by the way: far from perfect, but at least stable."

"Glad to hear." Sam stepped out and shut the doors. "Again, I appreciate your help."

Sam followed Doc into the house, through a side door that led to the kitchen.

Fried eggs, biscuits and coffee: simple, but the combination did fulfill.

"We need to get some food into your partner. Cassie fixes a fine dish. If we can get a portion into him, I got a feelin' he'd have a better chance toward recovery."

"Much obliged. Whatever you can do." Sam sipped his coffee, his cognition sharpening, along with the urge to head out. "You're Quaker, right?"

"How'd you know?" asked Cassandra, passing him another biscuit, which he declined.

"I say, it's obvious."

"More of that Indian instinct?" Doc winked.

"Maybe."

"From what tribe do you hail, Sam?"

"Not sure." He saw no reason to elaborate. "I got the blood in me. There's no doubt of that, but I'm not full Indian."

Doc placed his palm upon his heart. "Well, we are what we are—human. That suffices."

Sam nodded. "I won't argue that, though some men seem less human than others."

"I suppose in your bounty trade, you would see it that way."

"Sheriff Kendle—he's not Quaker. He said he fought in the war."

"Indeed, he's not Quaker, nor is Elroy. Paul was hired for his edge, though he's a fair man with an even temper. The combination meshes well with the Quaker ways. He's a Union man, as he said, though with relatives in the North and South. He chose the side that better fit his disposition. Elroy fought as well: the 54th Massachusetts Infantry Regiment, to be exact. Fought for his freedom, not to mention the chance to shed his name— the surname, that is, since it stemmed from slave attribution. Paul thinks quite highly of Elroy and vice versa, as I'm sure you've figured. They respect each other because they respect men who possess the same mettle, that need to put their lives on the line for principles."

"And yet among your town folk, there's reluctance when it comes to these raiders."

"These raiders have kept their distance, Sam. Why should we look for a fight, set the pace for some imagined requital? That for sure isn't the Quaker way."

"But what if they should bring the fight to you, as now seems likely?"

"Which is why we're strolling to Paul's this morning, to see what he's accumulated. If the council agrees to the cause—if our citizens do—they'll need to know how to handle the equipment. Hunting rifles and Bowie knives are fine for basic purposes, but it's another thing to take up a weapon and strike a man down—to strike a man dead, that is."

"It takes a hard heart to kill. I should know."

Sam's words chilled the couple, and in noticing this, he almost apologized.

Doc wiped his mouth, stood and kissed his wife. "We should be on our way." He patted Sam's shoulder. "What do you say, young man?"

"Yes, I'm ready." He gave Cassandra a bow. "Thank you for the fine breakfast, ma'am."

"You're welcome, Sam." Her eyes grew teary. "You be careful now—both of you."

Doc smiled. "Don't you worry, Cassie. We will."

Doc led the way, his gait slow but assured as he cut through the town's sidelines, entering a row of quaint houses.

Kendle and Elroy waited in the lawman's yard. The latter waved with marked impatience, ushering them to the boxy, gray structure that at first looked of little consequence, but upon closer inspection, one could see it was laden with crossed boards and heavy panels: a vault cloaked by wood.

"Looks bigger than I recall," Doc confessed. "Would give my ol' shanty barn some competition." He twirled his finger at its huge lock and chains. "So, you opening it or what?"

Elroy gave Kendle an exasperated huff, and the sheriff keyed the lock and yanked the chains like they were a couple steel snakes. He then swung the doors open and backed up with proud panache, exclaiming, "Behold, gentlemen, behold."

To say that Doc gasped would be an understatement, for the shed's walls were, in fact, bricked (the outer coating, therefore, a mere dressing) and jammed to the peak with rifles, muskets, pistols, knives and bayonets, some hanging from hooks and others stacked along long, wide shelves. There were bullets galore, clustered between the weapons and glistening from topless crates along the floor.

"Amazing." Doc removed his spectacles and rubbed his eyes. "It truly is an impressive stockpile."

Kendle reached in and grabbed a thick, dingy blanket that covered a bulky form. "You'd be surprised what one can amass over time."

Doc refastened his glasses and drummed his jaw as the object's large, discolored wheel was revealed. "Is that what I think it is?"

"Yep, Doc, it is. A genuine cannon: a Napoleon twelve-pounder, no less." Kendle kicked the wheel and caressed its bronze husk. "Elroy made a sweet deal for it. Got it through word of mouth. He even got the balls to go along with it, plus plenty of powder. As you can imagine, it was one hefty haul and not easy for Elroy to conceal along the way. Anyhow, some ol' rebel kid sold it to him. Cost a week of my wages, but I do believe it was worth it. The crass, little bastard told Elroy he wanted the money for some pretty, Italian harlot who frequents the Chesterfield Saloon. Sure hope he got his money's worth."

Under any other circumstances, Sam would have laughed, but was more interested in assessing the shed's other items. Sure, there was a lot, but what was its quality? How much of it, the twelve-pounder included, was even operational?

He moved to enter. "Do you mind?"

With a confident smile, Kendle gestured Sam to proceed.

With eagerness, Sam scrutinized the "merchandise." Most of it looked sturdy, even if on the whole, the contents were old and grainy.

Kendle eyed Sam. "What do you think? Good?"

"Sufficient." Sam stepped back. "Don't know if it'll be enough. By all accounts, these men have an arsenal to match any regiment. It's going to come down to whether everything is working condition, not to mention whether your men have the guts to use it."

With great conviction, Kendle affirmed, "They'll conjure whatever heart and soul is required do the job, and everything's been tested, all is in working order."

"The cannon, too?"

Kendle scratched his ear. "Okay, we didn't test the cannon, but I know my artillery, what's sturdy and what's not. Trust me, that device is in quality condition. Besides, it wasn't as if we could just fire it off without all hell breaking loose. In case you're unaware, those damn things are fairly noisy."

Sam still had his doubts but did not argue. He sensed the gamut of Kendle's restiveness, his understandable urge to succeed

Doc stepped away. "If the council should agree to take up arms, there'll be more than enough to go round. Even so, a show of heart will be the deciding factor." He wrung his hands. "I'll do what I can and insist we converge by dusk."

"You gotta make it happen, Doc," Kendle pleaded.

Doc nodded and then signaled Sam to accompany him, but as Sam turned, he noticed something peculiar in the second-floor window of Kendle's home: a little girl staring out at him, her cherubic countenance shrewd and attentive. He ascertained who she was and wondered why it seemed she had fixed her gaze on him. Was it his bronze skin and long hair that drew her?

In response, he wiggled his fingers in a half-hearted wave, but she fell from view.

"We'll saunter down the road, Sam," Doc suggested, "and then you're on your own. You know how to get back to my house, don't you?"

Sam wished he could stay with Kendle and Elroy, if only to help them determine strategic locations about town, but being too pushy could spook them. Heaven forbid they relegate him to the sidelines.

"I know the way, Doc." He noticed the doctor's slack jaw, the worry in his eyes. "Good luck to you, sir."

"Thank you, Sam. Most appreciated. If I do pull it off, you're going to need luck, too. The folks in this town have good hearts, but they can be stubborn. You'll have to be pretty persuasive to get them on board. You up for that?"

The idea unsettled Sam. 'I suppose."

"They might get accusatory. People tend to do that when they're scared."

Sam smiled, "I understand. I'll be as persuasive as I can. I promise."

They then parted ways, wary but no less determined.

CHAPTER EIGHTEEN

Perdifious hoisted the torch before the blood-stained doors and scanned those gathered.

Wrapped in sheets like a mummy, Crabby's carcass rested at Perdifious's feet, but he regarded it with concealed disrespect.

Under the bright sun, the men waited, impatient and irritable from the night's revelry. However, if their leader requested their attendance, who were they to argue? Insubordination was not worth the risk.

"Mister MacIntosh is dead—dead thanks to the vengeful intruders: a fancy-dressed scribe, an Indian and a famed, walking corpse. Perhaps this audacious trio was angered that we purged zealous Purity from the earth. Perhaps they wished to avenge those struck dead. If so, they came up short and yet left us this one sad casualty." Perdifious spread his arms and shook his head. "Despite it, we are strong—a legion for the greater cause of evil."

Somber silence spread, until someone felt compelled to whistle and cheer: the lunatic with the Confederate cap, his suit creased by blood and in his hands, the woman's bugged-eyed head, which he swung about.

"Hail, Perdifious," he shouted. "We are legion. We are legion. We are legion."

The lunatic's chant caught on fast, inspiring others to join in. Perdifious let them indulge for a spell, but then swished the torch to and fro, thus snuffing the uproar.

"Hear me, my judgmental recruits. No matter how great our number, I still consider Mister MacIntosh's death an act of war. What adds insult to injury, our beloved Mister Walsh has also gone missing. Is he a victim as well of these irreverent crusaders? Indeed, my acute intuition does tell me so."

The "Confederate" hissed and booed, but with a stern glance, Perdifious silenced him.

"Instinct tells me to lead by example. It tells me we should take what we want, only then to let it go. The world is our oyster, all for the bold taking and discarding. Our adversaries will press on, and we will follow. The air here remembers pain, purgation...fire. We will leave this town in ashes, not in tribute to Sherman's merciless march, but rather bygone Damnation. We will move on and find yet another town to poison. We will squander and scar it. And which town deserves this special plucking? Which one, that is, would our tricky trio dare choose?" He grinned knowingly. "I do believe it is named after a field of daisies, where another pious population has staked its righteous claim. It houses the precise sort of puritanical fools who would grant sanctuary to our avenging aggressors."

Perdifious placed the flame upon Crabby's corpse, which crackled and spurt.

He then stroked it against the doors of HADES, making the wood brown and blacken as it multiplied the flame.

"Let it burn—burn to the ground." For extra effect, Perdifious trembled. "We will leave this town in the dust from which it sprang. We will take our horses, wagons and weapons and spread as only we can, but this time it will be more than a symbol of the weak that we leave behind. This time we will savor the fruits of our labor. This time, we will toss the men into oblivion and defile their women and children for our utmost pleasure. We will discard their carcasses when we are through, all in the resplendent name of poisonous purgation."

Perdifious hurled the torch into the crowd, where it was caught and passed from man to man, structure upon structure ignited, more torches spawning from what burnt to ensure yet even more would burn.

The giggling lunatic followed Perdifious to his wagon and hopped atop, placing the head alongside him and then fingered the reins, the anticipating horses stirring and neighing as the pompous Perdifious occupied his perch.

The giggler waited for direction, but when none came, he asked with cautious uncertainty, "Straight forth, sir?"

"No," Perdifious replied, his tone as smooth as wine. "We'll veer west, off the beaten track."

"West, sir? Why?"

"Trust me." Perdifious's eyes twinkled. "There's much to see and much to find."

CHAPTER NINETEEN

FROM THE MIND OF RICHARD O'MALLEY:

I sensed a significant time had passed, despite my anaesthetized pain and through it; I have documented my words upon imaginary paper and folded them within my gray matter, in hopes that one day I might cull them from memory and transcribe them by rote. For now, I imagine that they just float about the air, anxious to land. Perhaps they will. Perhaps they won't.

You might like to know that my head hurt to the extreme. The throbbing at least prodded my cognition in an attempt to calm my coma. It also helped expand my mind, so that I could flee Palmer Perdifious's intrinsic spell and the cerebral pulsations that flowed from it.

In this respect, I did not feel a link to Sam, but something more encompassing. It touched upon activities that in one sense seemed distant in their meaning, and yet through the emotional waves they churned, my comprehension increased.

"Straight forth, sir?"

I saw—felt—the doctor wandering the daisy-laden town, asking reluctant officials to hear him out. Indeed, they would consent to a meeting, though only out of respect to one who had done right by them in those special times of need, but of course, they knew he acted as a mere messenger to someone they now only tolerated.

Sheriff Paul Kendle's lingering presence remained with me from the time he had visited my bed. I appreciated his desperation and would have risen to the occasion to stand by his side, if only I could have.

Now it was up to a supercilious coalition to endorse Kendle's intent: not an endeavor I envied, for I knew that even the most skilled elocutionist would have trouble shaking a Quaker's conviction.

Cindy darted toward Kendle as he headed for the door, but Emily tugged her back.

"Hold on there, young lady. You're staying here, tucked in bed. Mister Kendle will be home soon. Don't you fret."

Cindy stomped and whined.

"Why's she carrying on?' the sheriff asked. "As much as I'd like to take her, I'm afraid it would clutter the intent. It's not like she's willing to talk, after all."

Emily grabbed the child from behind and dragged her to the stairs. "That's enough, young lady." She glanced at her husband. "Go on, now. You don't want to be late."

He slipped on his hat and entered the warm air.

Cindy kicked and moaned as Emily ascended and then tossed her into the room.

"Put that nightgown on and get into bed. I mean it, now."

Cindy held her ground for a moment before feigning an air of calm. She walked to the chair where her night dress was draped and grabbed and pressed it to her chest.

Emily sighed and shook her head. "That's more like it. I'll visit in a bit. I want you under those covers when I get back."

However, no sooner had her guardian shut the door, Cindy bolted to the window. She looked upon the roof and estimated its slant and the distance it would take to reach the nearby, craggy tree. If she could reach the tree, she could balance herself upon its branches and then make her way down, but she had to move fast if she was to succeed.

She opened the window and with utmost care, ambled across the roof. She reached a begging branch, gripped it and swung herself down onto several others, digging her nails into the bark. Like a squirrel, she shimmied onward, tearing her dress and skinning her knees before hitting the grass.

Down the path, she spotted Kendle walking and with quiet vim, followed.

Smoke darkened the dusk sky, though few paid it much mind, in particular Doc, who contemplated upon the night's planned proceedings. Sam, on the other hand, could not shake the tormented wavers of gray and excremental lime. He could also smell the decomposing stench. It was distanced enough not to be a threat, but its implication still made him uneasy. If only he had the Dead Sheriff strutting with him, he may have felt more confident.

Men in black with wide-brimmed hats and a smattering of bonneted women in thick, dowdy dresses appeared along the trail. They offered gentle smiles, though their collective glint indicated staunchness.

Kendle met them along the way, quiet and somber as he neared. The same could be said of Elroy, who surfaced within close proximity of the humble, white church, his arms folded in pensive consternation. The two were as conspicuous as Sam among the conformist flow, their attire suiting their trades more than the setting.

"Once the folks are settled, I'll do the obligatory intros," Doc informed Sam as they approached the steps. "We'll hear the basic arguments. You'll talk thereafter. In this way, what you say will have more impact."

"I see." Sam's tone was flat.

"That's on Paul's recommendation, you know. He's been through this dance before. He thinks an outsider's view can sway the consensus better than our own: a good, grand finale." He glanced at Sam's waist. "Oh, and thanks for not coming armed. It's one thing for Paul to do so. It's his job, but for anyone else, particularly a stranger, well, it could send the wrong message."

Kendle and Elroy entered, removing their hats in unison with the others, the procession playing in a way that looked almost choreographed.

Chairs were aligned along the stage, a podium centering them. A small, round man slipped into a chair to the right, while a tall, bearded one occupied the chair to the left. They placed their hats under their chairs and folded their hands in pious positions, allowing Doc to direct the others to their assigned spots: Kendle and Elroy to the left; he and Sam to the right. However, it did not take long for the doctor to fidget, fanning himself with his hat and twisting about his seat, before deciding it was time to confront the podium. He donned a reluctant grin, which in its discomfiture quieted the assembly's murmurs. The tension remained palpable, stifling and strained.

"We are gathered here this evening," Doc declared, "on request of Sheriff Paul Kendle and with some hesitation, our council members. I appreciate their willingness to discuss a pressing concern, in light of recent events, which not all of you have been made aware of." Doc took a deep breath. "In the name of formality, I would like to introduce this meeting's participants."

Doc motioned to the small, round man. "We have Mayor Edward Pendrake in attendance." He then motioned to the tall, bearded man. "He is accompanied by Pastor George Ellis Leigh." Doc pointed to the front pew. "Also, gathered are our supporting members, of whom I am a part: the Honorable John Theodore Vincent of the Daisy Field Judiciary Branch, General Store Proprietor Raymond Pierce and Oliver Sloan of Sloan Banking Services." The elderly mustached trio rose and nodded. "Sheriff Paul Kendle is in attendance, along with Mister Elroy and as a guest on behalf of them and yours truly, Doctor Frederick Faraday—Mister, uh, Sam."

Tense whispering burst, but subsided as soon as Doc raised his finger.

"As you no doubt recall, we have had prior sessions concerning Sheriff Kendle's concern of a possible attack by belligerent nomads in or about our vicinity. It has been Sheriff Kendle's position that we should take precautionary measures, with a distribution of weaponry among our male population. At the last meeting of such concern, it was determined by unanimous vote not to act upon such. This position was not only embraced by the council but the general citizenry."

Pendrake and Leigh nodded in affirmation.

"Recent events have, however, led not only Sheriff Kendle and Mister Elroy to revisit the concern, but have inspired me to do so, as well. This decision is based on a couple concerns. The appearance of a distraught, little girl to our town being the first. She is yet to speak, but her disheveled appearance has led us to believe she was placed under great duress and is now under the guardianship of the Kendles. To intensify matters, we received an alarming visit from Mister Sam and his partner, Mister Richard O'Malley, a reporter for the Boston Globe, as I've been told. Mister O'Malley was captured, per Mister Sam's account, by the alleged nomads who have evidently settled in Purity." He rethought his choice of words. "'Invaded' is better verbiage than 'settled,'" if what Mister Sam conveys is accurate, and I have no doubt that his claim is. Mister Sam rescued Mister O'Malley from Purity's church, of all places, where Mister O'Malley was tortured and per my analysis, poisoned into unconsciousness. At present, the catatonic Mister O'Malley remains under my care."

Intense whispers resurfaced.

"Now, now," Mayor Pendrake blared, standing with his typical, roly-poly sway. "There is no need to rush to conclusions, my good people, regardless of what Doctor Faraday relays. Yes, the child's manifestation is, as I understand it, most peculiar, as is the situation with the disabled Mister O'Malley, but really, does either of it define a genuine threat? Even if Purity has been seized, that does not mean we are apt to suffer the same consequence. Washington can be notified and intercede if matters have truly progressed as reported."

Pastor Leigh then stood. "Mayor Pendrake makes a valid point. We are God-fearing people who adhere to God-abiding ways. New variables, which may or may not connect, give no cause for alarm or the need to bear arms. If we take such a drastic step, our convictions mean nothing."

Kendle's temper rose. He looked to Doc for permission to speak, but the cacophony in Leigh's favor had grown deafening. He rose and waved his gun.

Silence spread. "Um, Sorry for the scare, friends," Kendle stated with a brush of humility, "but as I've demonstrated, a show of might can keep control and instill a matter quickly. I said this before and I'm sayin' it again, Daisy Field is susceptible to attack. One way to attract an attack is to turn a blind eye to what rides on the horizon. This town isn't far removed from Purity in its ideology and ways, and something bad has evidently struck it."

"Purity's state of affairs is speculative," Mayor Pendrake scoffed.

"And besides," offered Pastor Leigh, "it was hampered by unorthodox practices right from the start. I know Winifred Wakefield well enough to call him a good-hearted acquaintance, but he always proved radical to a fault. From what I can recall, his flock does not dare engage even in the necessity of hunting, choosing instead to barter for goods. Perhaps Purity's populace reached out to the wrong individuals for the sake of such a trade. If such an exchange turned dire that would be a pity, but no reason for panic." He looked to his audience with jeering exasperation. "Besides, what would Sheriff Kendle have us do? It's not as if Daisy Field is any better equipped to ward off aggressors than Purity. More so, it's not our way to look for a fight, let alone stoke one." He raised a fist and tapped it into his palm. "As I am sure we can all agree, such action only results in more of the same. Threats, my dear citizens, beget threats. Violence begets violence. It's a frightful cycle that once initiated cannot be stopped."

Kendle's frustration beamed as brightly as his badge. Elroy suppressed his need to cuss, while Sam could only think of the deaths that he and the Dead Sheriff had caused in their many travels, but upon further reflection, he realized the meaning behind those deaths. Sometimes one had to fight—and kill—to right wrongs and when need be, keep others from harm. Kendle knew this, but failed to muster the expression.

"You can't bury your heads in the sand," he chastised. "You don't have an excuse anymore." He looked to Elroy, as if to say this was their big moment of reveal. "We have the ammunition, a whole shed of it, stocked from top to bottom. Elroy and I have been stashing it away, piece by piece, purchased from our own hard-earned funds." He pointed to the three men below. "I know you men hunt. I've seen you head out on those cold, Saturday morns. I know you know how to handle a rifle. It's not hard." He looked upon the rest of the audience. "I know every man here has the ability to point and fire if need be, and if not, you can be taught. I can teach you. Elroy can teach you. We got our hands dirty in the war, gained the necessary experience and know-how. We never enjoyed the thick of battle, striking other men down, but we did what we had to do. Anyone here can do the same. Being obedient to the Good Book is all nice and respectable, but it won't be enough to keep your families safe."

"You have no right to frighten us, Sheriff," some random Quaker cried.

"No right to make us feel guilty," another blared.

"Or feel like cowards," barked another.

More of them chimed in, all sputtering a variation of the same.

Doc looked to Sam. Perhaps now was the time for him to share his disturbing details.

Sam took a deep breath and walked to the stage's ledge, which in itself was enough to blunt the barrage, though rage remained on every face that beamed his way.

His throat quavering, Sam proceeded: "As Doctor Faraday has stated, my...my name is Sam. I'm a bounty hunter by trade." He saw several folks exchange circumspect exchanges. "My friend, Mister O'Malley is, indeed, a journalist. He's been documenting our, uh—that is, my exploits. On a passing basis, I've visited Daisy Field. On this most recent occasion, I was prompted by great urgency, in that Mister O'Malley was in dire need after I had rescued him. Doctor Faraday gave you the story."

Sam heard a few disbelieving yawns and wished he had practiced before opening his mouth.

"Anyway, Purity has been captured, taken over by these mad marauders. We first learned of the matter after a man—I would presume one of their ranks—mentioned it when he tried to rob us. When we did get to Purity, we heard a great commotion outside the town, which confirmed our fears, and—"

"We've heard all of this, dear sir." Judge Vincent then stood. "Must we endure a repeat? What we require is proof—substantial, irrevocable proof that we are in danger. Now, I will ask you, Mister Sam, can you supply it?"

Sam was offended by the snide demand. Instinct told him to leap down and smack the bastard into respectful submission, though he realized that would not have gained him any favor.

"Let him speak," Kendle scolded. "You should know the importance of hearing a man out, Your Honor."

"But again," retorted the judge. "I know his claim—heard it first off from the doctor this morn when he asked that I attend. I repeat, I do not wish a rehash. None of us do, Sheriff Kendle. I'd much prefer heading home to bed, and as for your alleged, procured ammunition, may it rot in Hell for all that I—or anyone here—should care."

"Agreed," chirped Mayor Pendrake and Pastor Leigh simultaneously.

As the matter grew more heated and folks converged from their pews to express their solidarity, Sam's mind swarmed, understanding the gamut of Kendle's frustrating burden.

Sam thought of the Dead Sheriff, of how impervious the corpse had made him feel during times of duress. He imagined the cadaver's swaying arms and shuffling feet and felt the immense though impractical need to show his companion's carcass to those gathered.

It was during this misguided reverie that he then noticed a small head bobbing forth, traveling along the church's outer, right side. When the wee figure shot toward the stage, he recognized the face—the little girl from the window.

Their eyes locked as the garrulous voices blended into a drawled hiss.

A spurt of unexpected thunder struck, followed by the sound of heavy rain. A windswept tap caused the church bell to ring.

Sam reached out to her on impulse, but his mind was in many places at once. Kendle also then spotted her.

"What are you doing here?" The sheriff pointed at her and looked about the church. "Where's Emily?"

The girl ignored him and maintained her gaze on Sam. The strange exchange soon caught the attention of others, to the point where all noticed. Silence fell.

Sam fanned his fingers, his beckoning strong enough to make her dash onto the stage, but once she ascended, she walked right past him and positioned herself before Doc, her back braced against the podium.

The rain drilled harder.

She opened her mouth, her lips trembling in a way that conveyed hesitation, but then in a frenetic burst, she unleashed a voice loud, clear and fiery:

"My parents—my parents are dead, killed by bad men you've been told about. You say you doubt that they could do you any harm, but I'm telling you, these men will harm you. They are real. Evil is real, and it's near. I watched people like you in a church just like this—all shot dead. I watched people young and old shot dead. I saw Pastor Wakefield shot dead. I saw the blood—all that blood everywhere." She raised her little hands and imagined the blood upon them. "I can still feel it—feel it all over me—and you say, you don't believe? You say you won't stand up? You won't fight." Her eyes bulged and her mouth twisted into a fierce frown. "You're as good as dead, then. Your families are as good as dead. These men will come for you. They're coming now. What happened to Purity was just the start. You wait and see. You're going to die. You're all going to die. Daisy Field is going to die, unless for God's sake you wake up."

A creeping numbness inundated the church. It rode on the child's unwitting incantation, seeping through Doc, Kendle and Elroy, washing over those below, flooding the pews, only then to swing back to the stage where the contagious, influencing atmosphere saturated Sam, making him for the moment drowsy. The little girl had accomplished something that the men could not. She had not only impacted an obstinate audience but penetrated a suppressive atmosphere with her distressed, spiritual thrust. A miracle it was, spawned through pure, purposeful persuasion.

"It's all right," Doc breathed, perhaps more to himself than the child. "It's all right, I say." He looked at the awestruck audience. "It appears we have a choice to make, don't we? It's a choice we may not wish to make, but it must be made. It must—"

"It must be made now," Kendle declared, sweat rolling off his brow.

Elroy added. "And if it's not now, then when? We know what this little girl says is true. It's got to be true. I feel it. You feel it, too, don't you?"

"Is it worth the risk of believing otherwise?" Kendle implored. "Is it?"

No one answered, and that, in itself spoke volumes.

Sam felt an inexplicable draw beyond the church. He then walked away, down the stairs and on through the center aisle, oblivious to who saw.

He opened the doors, leaving them ajar as he stepped outside, the rain only then ceasing. Down the street, he saw the Dead Sheriff, waiting as if for his command, a woman quivering across from the corpse, muttering, "Where are you? Where are you?"

It was Emily, her face ruddy and streaked, incapacitated by the zombie's rigid rot, a Colt grasped in his craggy hand, while the other hovered above his opposite holster.

"Everything's fine," Sam assured her, mounting his gait. "He won't hurt you." Sam cocked his thumb at the church. "I know who you're looking for. She's inside. She's safe."

He heard the pitter-patter of small feet, followed by those of adults.

Cindy ran to Sam's side, Kendle, Elroy and Doc on her heels.

The child looked up with eyes glistening, and to Sam acknowledged, "I know who you are." She turned and pointed to the corpse. "I know who he is, too."

Emily found the courage to dash over, but no sooner had she budged, her husband brushed by her and headed straight for his crusty counterpart.

"So, it's true." With wide eyes, Kendle paused before the towering shape and held his nose to repress a gag. "So, it's not a man in a mask. It's goddamn real."

"Yeah," Sam whispered, "as real as you or me, except dead and yet living."

Sam concentrated, and the Dead Sheriff returned his Colt to his holster. From there, Sam made a quick, shaman-like motion, and the cadaver turned.

"I'm sorry for this," Sam murmured, hoping his tone rang true, but was he apologizing for the Dead Sheriff, his lack of articulation in the church or bringing danger upon the town? No doubt it was all of the above.

People noticed the looming, shadowy shape as they neared, but they were not close enough to sense anything amiss. From their vantage, the Sheriff could have been anyone, even one of their own. Still, Sam could not risk dampening their zeal with something they would brand evil. "We're heading back to Doc's. I know you have questions, and I—that is, the Dead Sheriff and I—can answer them."

As Sam and the Sheriff progressed down the path, Emily grabbed Cindy and held her close, while the church members layered Kendle, Elroy and Faraday with questions.

"How many guns do you have?"

"Can you teach us to use them?"

"Is it better to wound or outright kill a man?"

The council stood on the outskirts, listening, their expressions grave, their hesitation fueled.

Indeed, Daisy Field may have gained a fighting chance against the inevitable, but even with the collective position erected, the task ahead would still remain cataclysmic.

CHAPTER TWENTY

"What's that?" Perdifious asked, swiping some raindrops from his vest. "Slow the wagon. Slow all the wagons."

With one hand cupping his sweet, severed head, the giggler pointed. "A body? Yep, yep, that's what it is—a body."

Perdifious slapped the henchman's shoulder and gestured him to halt and then inspect.

The giggler made certain his head was neatly arranged before leaping off and from there snickered his way toward the scrawny body in faded black. He grabbed a stick and poked its fly-swarmed frame, jostling it just enough to reveal its face.

"Walsh—it's Walsh, Mister Perdifious." He tossed the stick to the side, knelt and lifted the body by the front of its shirt, so that its face became visible under the burgeoning starlight. "Looks like he was shot—shot right in the forehead."

Perdifious inhaled the humidity and tossed it back per raised tonality. "Yes, Mister Walsh has been shot—shot dead. Oh, the audacity. I do wonder who may have committed the horrid deed?" He thought of his recurring premonition and what it truly meant, having always feared its intent. Now, thanks to this fortuitous opportunity, the meaning was clear. "Who, indeed?"

Murmurs spread. Horses moved to the front. The giggler turned the body to and fro, giving ample angles so the men could verify its identity.

With contemptuous zeal, they barreled forth, each taking an impulsive yet cathartic turn at tearing into the dead general, ripping at his clothes and then his limbs. The giggler's enthusiasm grew ever louder and others laughed along with him.

The mad snapping and tearing hit its crescendo: a rich, symbolic culmination aimed at those who committed the deed, but also in honor of the man who helmed their wicked endeavors.

With Walsh's remains reduced to mush, Perdifious instructed the giggler to hush, and so then did the rest. The tight-lipped giggler snorted back to his seat, wiggling alongside the head. Perdifious gave an instructive nod. The wagon progressed.

No words were needed to underscore the ultimate intent. The die had been cast, the poison injected. Daisy Field's fate would be assiduous, sadistic and per Perdifious' warped aspiration, a matter of impure perfection.

The Dead Sheriif's dogged eye gleamed by candlelight. Though the corpse's rot still disturbed him, Kendle weathered it, listening to the thing's breathing, but of course, it did not breathe.

Was it some sort of mechanized puppet? Kendle had once encountered such a contraption at a carnival in Fairfax County, Virginia (long before the war was a glint in anyone's eye), but that was but a small, spindly harlequin aimed to please children, not some towering, grimy husk. No, there was something more to this mammoth form than met the eye. It was real all right, but in what precise way?

"So, he's dead yet alive, you say?"

Sam sat on the hay, his face shadowed, despite the flickering chunks of wax that Doc had placed about the ground. Sam did not answer, leaving the response to his vicarious cadaver.

"I am dead yet alive, Sheriff Kendle." The Dead Sheriff's voice was gruff and intimidating, his mouth moving like a ventriloquist's dummy. "I have risen from the grave to avenge all wrongs, no matter the time, no matter the place."

"And that's why you came upon Daisy Field? To avenge a wrong—a potential wrong, perhaps?"

The Sheriff's leathery throat bobbed and creased, "I came to save O'Malley."

"So, you work for O'Malley and Sam?"

"They work me. O'Malley writes our stories. Cheveyo helps me hunt."

"Cheveyo? Who's Cheveyo." Kendle looked at Sam. "That you?"

Sam shrugged, taking quiet delight in the confession. "Yeah, in certain circles."

Doc snapped his fingers. "I do recall the Dead Sheriff's companion going by that name—Cheveyo. None of these prime crusaders use their real names, you know. The same would go for their sidekicks." He looked at the Dead Sheriff and cringed. "At least Sam and Dead Sherriff aren't of the foppish sort. I can't say it enough. If you're gonna strike fear into outlaws, renegades and like, it's best to avoid that powdery fluff."

Kendle shook his head and scanned the Dead Sheriff further. "Gotta say, I didn't expect anything this frightening. It's one thing to get folks off their asses with a good scare, but the Dead Sheriff adds a whole other layer to the matter."

"Not a bad thing, I suppose," Elroy remarked.

The Dead Sheriff's mouth cranked open. "I am here to help."

"See?" Elroy snapped his fingers. "He's here to help, and we need all the help we can get."

Kendle was still wary. "With all due respects, I don't know what to make of this. I don't mean to sound like one of my judgmental detractors, but if this character is undead, I can't imagine it's the result of something divine. It's gotta come from the opposite end." He glanced at Sam. "Is that the case, Cheveyo?"

The question struck a chord, but Sam stayed stoic. "The Dead Sheriff said he would help. That should suffice."

"It's gotta suffice," Elroy argued. "Let's make do with what we've got, Paul."

"I agree," chimed Doc. "God has a way of working things out. If this, uh, Dead Sheriff has made his way to us, regardless of the particulars, I say we take what he offers and be glad for it." He scanned the corpse. "Isn't that right, Sheriff?"

"Yes," the Dead Sheriff answered.

Kendle groaned. "Why'd he come to the church?"

"Curiosity," the Dead Sheriff gurgled.

"Armed and ready, too," Kendle quipped, "but for what?"

Sam did not like where the inquiry was going.

"Why did he come to the church?"

The corpse retorted, "Anything and everything that is bad, Sheriff Kendle."

Kendle considered the reply and after a tense pause, sighed. "Anything and everything. I suppose that's what we can expect, and yet, I wouldn't mind being proven wrong. I truly do hope these men never come. I hope that the federal government does intervene and grants justice for whatever bad was done. I hope and pray it works out that way, and yet I do have my doubts. I do have my fear and my hate, and it's based on lots of things I wish I could forget." He stared hard at the Dead Sheriff. "I only hope that I—that all of us—can make a difference if things do hit the point of no return. You understand, don't you, Sheriff?"

The Dead Sheriff nodded.

Sam leapt from the hay and headed over. "Even the Dead Sheriff needs his rest. I'm putting him to bed, now. He's expressed himself more than enough for one night. Rest assured, he's on our side. When need be, he'll fight the good fight, as we all will."

As Sam guided the Sheriff to the wagon, Elroy pulled Kendle to the side and waved Doc toward them.

"You gotta maintain your focus, Paul," Elroy whispered, though Sam managed to absorb each syllable. "This is like something out of a dream, a nightmare, but it also seems fated. For whatever reason, the tide truly has shifted, my friend. Something extraordinary is happening. We all know it. We're breathing it in. It's part of us, now. Men are counting on us cause of it. They'll be lined up at your home in the morning, ready to try those weapons. We've got to keep them on track. It'll be basic maneuvers that we'll share, if that even, but it'll be enough to get them comfortable and more so focused. They'll look to us for guidance, especially you, Paul. You can't flinch, not once, no matter how strange this gets."

"I'm fine, Elroy." Kendle donned a steely glint. He regarded his friend with confidence and passed it on to Doc. He then glanced back at the wagon, studying the way the ghastly shape slipped into the casket, so smooth and carefree for something so big and bulky. He watched Sam pat the thing's chest and watched Sam turn, so that the two shared a nervous, if not undetermined exchange.

"I'm ready—ready for whatever comes our way," Kendle buzzed under his breath. "Anything and everything, that is."

CHAPTER TWENTY-ONE

Men covered Kendle's property, most positioned about the shed. The sooty sky made some squint and sniffle. It was a distraction that Kendle could have done without, and Sam, though now accustomed to the foreboding effect, felt much the same. Concentration was imperative.

Sam also had another concern. He had visited O'Malley that morning; a compassionate gesture, but perhaps not the wisest move. To see his friend still unconscious caused more fright in Sam than rage, no matter what positive assessment Doc shared.

Sam considered Elroy's words, in particular the shifting tide. It was an apt description and no doubt the cause behind why Sam had subconsciously summoned the Dead Sheriff to the church.

"You pull the trigger," Kendle instructed, "and you shoot." He fired into the ground as a spry Quaker leaped before him, cupping his ears. "See there? That simple."

From the second-floor window, Cindy gazed once more at Sam. Their eyes locked. Again, he attempted a wave, but she ducked from sight.

At least folks knew her name now. Since her influential declaration, she had become quite the chatterer, or so he had been told. Perhaps it was good to keep her visible. After all, she was the reason these otherwise reluctant men showed today.

Kendle fired again into the ground. He received applause this time and looked yonder. "Say how bout that tree?"

As Kendle led the men to the object of practice, the council appeared, silent through it all, perhaps hoping that the exercises would not leave a permanent blemish on their community.

To Sam, the council's lack of enthusiasm meant nothing. The only one among them with any sense was Doc, and he was no doubt now an official castaway. Perhaps, though, it was good that the pompous asses had wandered in. Maybe they would learn a thing or two from what they saw, get prepared in their own right for when hell did come rushing in.

Kendle squinted and fired. Wood splintered. He smiled and handed the gun to the spry Quaker and positioned him to aim. The young man trembled, but whether through luck or innate skill gained success. Applause ensued. The gun was passed to another who also shot and succeeded, and then another.

Elroy, meanwhile, spoke of tactical concepts to a sideline group, essaying the best way to use rifles, muskets and bayonets. He also offered a few pointers regarding cannon fire. Those gathered were most impressed.

"So, we need to stop them from entering," Doc commented to Elroy. "I suppose that's the key."

"Elroy's brow wrinkled, as he slipped into thought. "It is, Doc. Paul has more than a few ideas regarding such. He'd like to fortify passages and dig trenches, but it's a matter of time, and time we don't have. If we have to rush, then we'll make good with what we got and be happy with it."

"But against an army?" Doc lamented. "That'll be tough."

"A small army, with not much more experience than our men have," Elroy surmised, concealing his doubt. "I bet we have more than enough men to match em."

"But our men haven't tasted blood, Elroy." Doc regarded the doughy expressions of those who dared eavesdrop. "What of that?"

"Anybody can taste blood." Elroy dragged his tongue across his teeth. "It only takes a drop to change one's perspective. Then instinct kicks in. It goes the same for any man. I know. I've seen the best and the worst get that taste. Paul has for sure. No one's immune to meeting the challenge when one's life is put on the line. And don't forget. Our men fight on the side of good. That's a big advantage in any conflict."

Little by little, the men received their weapons. They practiced and imagined what they would do when that pivotal time came.

Wagons entered the town's square. Sooner or later they would begin their exodus to Peach Water. A few men would go along with the women and children, just to be on the safe side, in the event the raiders cut into their trail.

The rest of the plan rode on speculation and lots of hope, while the ghosts of Purity hid inside the soiled air, anticipating release and praying that no others joined their stagnant ranks.

"The ashes point the way," the giggler snickered. "The wind directs them to Daisy Field. It's right around the bend, Mister Perdifious, itchin' for the pickin'." He cuddled his pet head. "Look, Matilda—look. A new town beckons." He rocked the head like a baby before kissing its blackened lips. "Sure would be nice if I found you a friend."

Perdifious found the suggestion sweet and played along. "Matilda is a redhead, unless her hair is merely dyed by blood. It's rather hard to tell. Still, a blonde or brunette would make her a fine companion."

The giggler wiggled with excitement. "Perhaps one of each, sir. Triplets sure would be real nice."

Perdifious laughed and patted his companion's back. "Now, that's the spirit. Oh, how I do admire your amorous ambition, Mister Giggler."

Two men on horseback approached. Perdifious had sent them ahead of the caravan to scope Daisy Field's expanse. .

"They've got guns," one conveyed.

"And they're firin' 'em," the other added. "Awfully odd for damn Quakers."

Perdifious smirked and responded loud enough for his men to hear. "I am pleased that they're not oblivious like Wakefield's flock. General Walsh's demise was but another indicator of that. I welcome the hostility and the subsequent challenge. It pre-seasons our pillaging."

"Oh, and that Indian you inquired about," the first scout stated. "There's only one Indian I could see, so it must be him."

Perdifious grinned further. "Perfect. Thank you for the confirmations, my faithful scouts."

The duo then joined the queue as Perdifious's wagon resumed its regal lead.

"Adapt a gradual pace," he instructed the giggler. "We'll strike later than sooner but keep it all within a practical timeline. I prefer these fools sleep on their perceived prowess. Let them believe they're valiant and pre-pared for a spirited face-to-face. That's their fate: too much faith, all too little, all too late."

Daisies soon appeared among the grass, but to Perdifious they were little more than fanciful weeds; frosting for the anxious poison beneath.

Perhaps the Master would dismiss his perception as overconfident, but his demons whispered the truth, etching it inside his head with each inch forward. Another Hades would be born and then another and another, until all the frosting on Earth had been licked way. He would stand as its Lucifer equivalent: an all-consuming, terrestrial evil that not even an amulet-bound Master could rival.

Anything and everything, Perdifious, thought, not knowing from where the words stemmed, only that they made sense.

Night fell.

Somewhere during his pseudo slumber, Sam heard O'Malley mumbling. Did the Faradays not hear? Surely, they would not let the poor man carry on so.

The whimpering then subsided. Had he imagined it?

He heard hooves and coarse wheels grinding and sloshing, moving ever closer, only to slow to a menacing crawl, pinging like tortuous blood upon Sam's brain.

He sensed another portion of the sky darken with a last puff of sickening soot and heard hard thunder even though he knew there was none.

His gut shifted and turned. The amulet grew cold, then warm.

He cracked his knuckles. The Dead Sheriff cracked his and rapped the casket.

Sam imagined the thoughts of the men in town, from Doc to Kendle, to Elroy to the council members to every man who now held a gun, and believed he could shoot with precision and maybe, if the good Lord willed it, without consequence.

For better or worse, this was the beginning of the end.

Sam closed his eyes and waited.

CHAPTER TWENTY-TWO

Someone knocked, the sound soft and small, like a bird pecking. Sam ambled forth and opened the doors, surprised to find Cindy standing there, though her gaze cut past him, falling upon the wagon and the hint of the coffin within.

"Say, what are you doing here?"

She moved her gaze up at him. "It's happening. It's happening now."

Her cold proclamation disturbed Sam.

"You got to go back to the Kendles. They'll be worried."

Doc appeared from the side, his frown long and fretful. "She's right, Sam. It's started." He grabbed the girl's hand, pulled her near. "We've been looking for her, you know. Paul had the women board the wagons, but only a few rolled out. The entire town is surrounded. Those bastards crept up, blocked us in. Emily's still here. She's in the house with Cassie. Cassie didn't want to leave, either. Maybe it's just as well, considering the way things fell. The gals can comfort one another in any event." Doc patted Cindy's head in a way that said he was sorry. "Gave my six-shooter to Cassie, just in case. I'll get another when I head back to the square. I've been told the leader of the opposition is waiting at the northern end, at the town entrance. Supposedly, he wants to fire upon whatever sneaks into sight, but he also has an offer, some sort of compromise." Doc paused and pointed at the barn. "Your boss—he'll make an appearance, right?"

"He'll be there." Sam wondered, though, how he might pull off the stunt. Should the Sheriff march straight in, guns ablazin' or wait in the shadows for a precise moment to strike? "You do what you need to, Doc. I'll be right behind. I'm sure Sheriff Kendle has everything under control."

Doc nodded and ushered the girl along, only to glance back. "We're counting on you—both of you." With a gentle push, he guided Cindy into the house, and then a few seconds later, re-emerged to give Sam a supportive wave and then shot down the road.

"Wait—hold up, Doc"

Doc turned, as Sam pointed into the barn.

"Why walk? The wagon's ready to roll, and I even have a stack of loaded guns to share." He smiled, even though he was wracked by doubt. "And you, my friend, have the first pick."

Kendle eyed the top of the bakery, where a Quaker was stationed at the window, rifle poised. Another armed Quaker was stationed across the way in the upper dress-shop window. Kendle tipped his hat at the men and then directed his horse a few yards downward.

Sam and Doc arrived to see other wagons lined up. Inside, weeping women and children peered out, too afraid to exit in the event of possible gunfire. However, a few of the braver ones did slip out, in evident hopes of finding safer pastures. Several men accompanied them, their bodies taut, their rifles cocked.

Elroy made his way over and focused on Sam, if only in that he had been out of the burgeoning loop. "Bad idea to have the procession start here, but that's where most of the wagons were clustered. Paul figured they could fan out from any number of angles and converge later, but these bastards moved in fast. Our wagons—the women and children—might as well be sitting ducks at this point. Some giggling fool out there made that known to us."

Sam grimaced and then steered the wagon alongside the general store. He hopped off and into the rear, where he tossed Doc a sack stuffed with his guns. "Give those to whoever needs them," he instructed the doctor and then returned to Elroy.

"At least things are in motion on our end," Sam offered.

"We do have men stationed all around," Elroy assured him. "If only we could've fortified it better. My heart goes out to Paul. He really wanted this done right. He sure tried."

"You've both done fine, Elroy."

Sam watched Doc hand the guns to the eager Quakers. When the weapons were depleted, he approached Kendle, who looked down at his friend, his expression haggard and drained.

"Doc told me the opposition has an offer."

"That's the claim, Sam. Comes from this fellow named Perdifious—scarred-up gent with a scraggly beard."

"I know who he is. The Dead Sheriff knocked him out cold when we rescued O'Malley. We should have killed him right then and there, but why draw attention? Damn, stupid move. That's for sure."

"Well, what's done is done. Here we are. We'll hear what he says."

Kendle galloped closer to the town's cusp. Men followed him, as did Elroy and Sam.

Perdifious's wagon was situated a few yards beyond, a long queue of less fanciful ones behind it, aligned with a number of men on horseback. Seated next to Perdifious was what may have passed for a Confederate court jester and a sadistic one at that, considering the grotesque object propped on his knee. The deranged dolt giggled, but his commander silenced him with a soft slap to his mouth.

Kendle sat up straight and glared at his stately aggressor. "You've been carrying on about an offer. That's what my men tell me anyway. What do you propose?"

Perdifious tugged his beard, pretending to think the matter over. "What do I propose? A good question, sir, but before I detail the conditions, introductions are in order."

Kendle's patience waned. "I've no time for games. State your case."

The giggler pinched his lips and drummed the top of his prop, while Perdifious paused and then with smug flair, declared, "I am Palmer Pedifious, conqueror of a small town called Purity. I decided to rename it, and then let Hades burn to the ground." He glanced upward. "I'm certain you noticed the smoke: my handiwork, of course. And you are, sir?"

"Paul Kendle, sheriff of Daisy Field."

"Daisy Field—yes, I do see how this ambrosial expanse was named.

Daisies are everywhere, but to me daisies are but little more than vibrant weeds. Weeds are meant to be uprooted, so that others may rise in their place. Such has become my new occupation—weed killer, weed restorer. All quite allegorical, you see."

"Get to the goddamn point, Perdifious," Kendle demanded.

Perdifious nodded. "I want the Dead Sheriff, but as much so, the Indian. I know the two are here. You may keep the dying dandy. He's no longer of use to me."

Kendle glanced at Sam, who waited for the sheriff's response.

"No deal," the lawman bellowed, spurring a rush of murmurs from both sides.

Perdifious looked insulted yet pleased. "With all due respects, Sheriff Kendle, I have given you the means to leave your Daisy Field unscathed. I do promise that if you grant my request, I'll have no reason to invade."

"You're a goddamn liar. You'll do to Daisy Field what you did to Purity, whether I comply or not. That's obvious."

"That Indian is no innocent, you must know. There's no doubt that he— or the Dead Sheriff—killed two of my highest-ranking men. I and my soldiers came upon evidence of one of their bodies, and we don't take kindly to a compatriot being left to decay on some lonesome trail. If you don't fulfill my request, we'll demonstrate our displeasure in ways that you cannot imagine, Sheriff Kendle. Are you willing to accept the consequences?"

Kendle held his ground. "I said no deal."

Perdifious relished Kendle's stubborn stance, but the council members edged toward him, the mayor muttering, "For the benefit of us all, his offer may be worth consideration."

Sam knew it was pointless to hand himself over to Perdifious, but it would have been strange if he did not at least go through the motions.

"I'll surrender." Sam slinked past Pendrake. "I'll hand myself over."

Kendle respected Sam's offer, but pointed to the wagon and its conspicuous casket, his eyes twinkling. "If you do that, Sam, where's that leave him?" He lowered his voice to a whisper. "Where's that leave us?"

Perhaps Kendle understood Sam's relationship with the Dead Sheriff more than he had let on.

"He is willing to go, Sheriff," Pendrake implored. "Why hesitate or would you prefer that I negotiate the terms?"

Kendle did his best to keep his temper. "No, sir, I would rather that you not and for what it's worth, you ought to be ashamed of yourself. It's one thing to turn the cheek, quite another to sacrifice a man in the vain hope of saving one's hide."

"I'm waiting," Perdifious exclaimed. "We can settle this now, Sheriff Kendle, no blood spilt. Unlike Purity, your flimsy sanctuary will stand. I will not ask again. Your answer, please."

Kendle unleashed a barrage of expletives, which Perdifious's men matched and rivaled. The giggler, meanwhile, notched upward, swinging his head around by its roots.

"I won't change my mind, Perdifious. My answer stands and all the consequences that come with it."

The declaration was then sealed. The air screamed for battle and pierced every man stationed on either side.

Kendle looked to the building tops, his eyes shifting from side to side, the men above tense and terse as they aimed downward.

Perdifious's parade bolted without warning, men yowling, guns blazing.

Kendle's horse reared. The men fired from above in a sloppy spree. As Perdifious's army stampeded, its members fired upward, knocking the man from the bakery to the ground, his weapon skidding beneath the rushing hooves. The man in the dress shop was also struck and stumbled backward, moaning and cupping his squirting shoulder.

"Fire, fire, fire," Kendle cried, turning his horse about, shooting a number of the enemy from their saddles as they neared, but it was Perdifious he wanted, but then, so did Sam.

The Daisy Field wagons broke into various directions, becoming unwitting if not convenient obstacles. Sam danced around them, focusing on his own. With his mind, he tapped the casket, summoning the Dead Sheriff to rise.

As the Dead Sheriff rose, Sam kept an eye on Perdifious, watching as his Confederate clown wheeled their wagon around. Reckless, yes, and to a less intuitive eye, perhaps suicidal. However, Sam discerned the manner in which the wind had bent and twirled. Cloaking Perdifious were gossamer demons, winged, horned and clawed.

As the wagon continued to circle, bayonet-geared assaulters barged in single file, stabbing the panicked Quakers. Their guts spilled onto the street, bullets zinging every which way, as Perdifious and his henchman gawked with glee, but in the harried process, Kendle managed to shoot the hat from the madman's head. The villain, however, remained undismayed, his scars pulsing with each rapid turn as he aimed in blame not at Kendle, but Sam. It was Sam he wanted. It was Sam, after all, who possessed the amulet.

KKKAAABBBOOOMMM!!!

The cannon ball rammed Peridifous's wagon, knocking it onto its side. Elroy stood behind the mighty machine, its wheel wobbling loose, rolling toward Perfifous's soldiers, who cowered anticipating another blast.

In the dusty aftermath, Sam lost track of his foe, but saw the headless body of the giggler, as the woman's head rolled toward his neck, a look of shut-eyed placidity upon her bruised face. Sam savored the sick irony.

Meanwhile, the wagon's splintered remains inspired the standing Quakers to renew their vigor. Without missing a beat, they fired upon their knife-wielding chargers and to those with guns, beat each to the trigger-pulling punch.

"Where is he?" Kendle cried, bullets striking his horse, which slumped with a pitiful neigh. "Where's Perdifious?" He slid from the saddle of the poor, dying beast and inched his way up, his eyes and pistol ticking from left to right. "Show yourself, you goddamn son of a bitch."

Doc crept behind his friend. "Be careful, Paul. Be careful. He could be anywhere, that tricky devil."

A devil, indeed, thought Sam, but even if Perdifious was motivated by some demonic drive, he was still bound by flesh and blood. .

Sam hunkered, raised his pistol and searched, determined to blow the man's skull to kingdom come. Beneath the zinging bullets, he detected his opponent's freakish aura along the side of another overturned wagon. Women and children had slid from out it, each shot dead, weeping men now kneeling before them. The display increased Sam's rage and perhaps because of it, a perplexing vantage overtook him, snapping his perspective in two.

He felt the Dead Sheriff marching, Colts hoisted as the flaking form stepped toward hazy center stage. As Daisy Field's valiant continued to fire and fall, the corpse shot their adversaries at every ponderous turn. Upon seeing the living dead man, the Quakers reeled, while Perdifious's men bombarded the apparition with all they had, but to no avail.

Sam's focus sharpened further in its miraculous, twofold way, leaving one side of his mind on Peridfious, who scooted among the passing horses and opposing onslaughts, skidding a few feet from the cannon that Elroy had repositioned, its wheel re-attached and fuse sizzling.

KKKAAABBBOOOMMM!!!

More of Perdifious' men hit the ground, their limbs twisted and severed from the massive blow. Elroy jumped and cheered, while the zealous villain edged ever near.

"Watch out, Elroy," Sam shouted, but no sooner had Perdifious crept inward, the bastard vanished.

Sam placed his palm upon the amulet, as Elroy tossed him a confident glance. Sam then stepped over the strewn body parts and wondered what another blow might bring, but at such time, the cannon collapsed, both wheels now unhinged. Without the proper mounting, its use had been spent.

Elroy cursed and cried, while Sam moved to and fro, his mind still orchestrating the Dead Sheriff's finesse, making him shoot and reload again and again, his crusty fingers popping bullets from his belt, nailing men from every angle, rejecting what they administered through long puffs of defiant soot and springing bile.

Suddenly, Perdifious sprung from the side, kicking Sam off his feet. Sam struggled to rise, as Perdifious rammed his heel into the Indian's wrist and reached for his chest.

In desperation, Sam harnessed the Sheriff with all his mental might, spinning the corpse around. The Sheriff aimed for Perdifious, but in a surreal move, the bastard stepped back and regarded the corpse with a combination of awe and fear. He only needed to shoot Sam dead, snatch the Master's pendant and flee. Why then did he pause? What was it about this resurrected quiddity that wracked and transfixed him so?

The Dead Sheriff extended his Colt, aiming for Perdifious's brow. Perdifious's heel pressed harder upon Sam's wrist, making the Indian wince and with this, the Sheriff stiffened. When he then fired, the bullet zinged past Perdifious's ear. Another grazed his collar, leaving the madman to retreat, wondering how many times would he come so close and yet fall so short of his goal?

Sam forced himself upward. The Sheriff's spine cracked and straightened, his desquamated hips whipping from side to side.

Bang! Bang! Bang! More raiders fell. Sam's indignation fueled the corpse's every move to the extent that the Dead Sheriff appeared to have a will of his own, and perhaps, if only based on his amazing, deft dexterity, he did. This left Sam to continue tracking his crafty adversary with transfixed focus.

Destiny dictated each opponent's actions. Destiny doomed them both, just as it had Purity, just as would Daisy Field.

CHAPTER TWENTY-THREE

FROM THE MIND OF RICHARD O'MALLEY:

I may have died for all I knew, but my spirit, detached and floating, felt renewed enough to dominate an astral plane.

I hovered above Mrs. Faraday and her visitors. The doctor's wife placed a gun beneath a folded cloth upon the bureau, away from child's view. It was a reassuring move in light of the suppressive doom. I heard Mrs. Faraday whisper a prayer. She needed the strength to survive—for all of us to do so—no matter how numbing the circumstance.

The overriding tension stilted me, and so it came to the child to pacify me. Through her gentle presence, I realized the women stayed with me due to this cherub's insistence. This was the only way Cindy would stay put, though I could not figure why she needed to stay so close, until her thoughts found a way to saturate mine, revealing the tenuous link that tied her misfortunate to mine.

I am uncertain if she envisioned any of my torture, but I could certainly see the river of blood that ran through Purity's church. I felt the weight of her parents upon me and experienced the anguished means to which this poor child had pushed from beneath them, the confounding panic and contempt that ensued upon her trek.

Her screeching pain forced my mind's eye to open. The sensation felt similar to when I had been chained to the ceiling and prodded so viciously. At such time, I had screamed from out my mind for Sam to arrive, but for this unconscious moment, I was uncertain to whom or what I dared summon. Then a jolting notion engaged me. I was not summoning anyone per se. Peridfious, on the other hand, was summoning me.

A part of him had, after all, remained within my brain. In fact, his underhanded presence seemed more tangible now. I wished him nowhere near me, but his penetrating spirit seemed to hook upon mine like sharp claws, my mind a mollified magnet to his attentive steel.

I prayed that the sickening sensation was but a figment of my accursed imagination, for if not, what then would come of me, whether dead or by some miraculous means, alive? If the former were to be the case, what then would become of these dear ladies?

Perhaps my current condition was synonymous with the doom I had prophesied, that thing that beckoned me when I looked to the sky and breathed the soured air. I should have taken more heed in what was un-

...why she needed to stay so close...

folding, but what was the point of regretting it now?

If only I could have reversed the revolting process, I would have done so, but I was trapped—trapped to wait and waver within my trenches of uncertainty. The feeling was so suppressive, in fact, that not even the culmination of the Master's hounding influence or Sam's bloody bounties could compare, and so with hope seemingly vacant, I anticipated a possible, if not probable, end to all ends.

Sam's vantage turned kaleidoscopic, his actions shackled to some diaphanous force.

Either side had an equal chance of winning, but considering the losses incurred, would there be any true winner? What now transpired was bloodshed for the sake of bloodshed.

Still, Sam would not resign the hunt. He knew Perdifious would strike again. He had to be ready somehow, someway.

He heard wagons attempting to exit and enter, the men from both factions growing sparser as he pressed on. Did that mean he had passed Perdifious in the rush? Had the Dead Sheriff slumped to the ground in the mind-bending interim, freed from Sam's thoughts?

Grass and trees rolled before him. Short, twining trails beckoned. Houses appeared, the landscape growing more familiar. Yes, he recognized the path, but was it wise to return to his base? Perdifious would not go there, would he?

Sam felt the villain's shadow bobbing, zipping from tree to bush and bush to tree as he gripped his pistol to the point that his knuckles turned white. The tension was that thick, that penetrating.

"All right, you weasel," Sam seethed, "why lure me here?" but then he recalled O'Malley's mystical malady. Had his friend not lured him toward Purity's church? Of course, the mad magician yet maintained a link with his friend. Perdifious could inflict further harm onto O'Malley in this respect, perhaps even kill him this time, not to mention the ladies of the house; Mrs. Faraday, Mrs. Kendle and of course, that sad, embittered, little lass, Cindy Brown.

Perhaps he had fallen into Perdifious's trap, but Sam sensed that the fiend was not yet inside. Perhaps he could prevent the scoundrel from entering.

"I know you're out there, Perdifious." Sam's tone was cold and direct. "I know what you're planning. It won't work. Face me like a man—face to face, gun to gun, a duel to the death. That's what you want, isn't it? If you win, you get the amulet. You get it all, Perdifious."

A long, insect-trilled pause followed and then the madman leapt up, his shadow unfurling from the trees. He fired, the bullet missing Sam's head by mere inches. In turn, Sam fired back and heard frantic shuffling.

"Come out, Perdifious. Fight or surrender, one or the other."

Perdifious fired again. Sam was set to reciprocate, homing in on the bullet's emanation, when another zinged past his head, though this time from behind. Startled, Sam turned and saw the Dead Sheriff.

The corpse had positioned his Colt to match Sam's stance, but the Sheriff's head was cocked back, and so Sam had to guide him into proper, dueling position. Again Sam called, "Come out, Perdifious. Come out where we can see you. The Dead Sheriff is here. He knows you're there."

Sam heard more shuffling and caught a glimpse of Perdifious's panicked face as he swooped toward the porch, a hint of surrounding, flapping wings and horns. So much for evil's shielding protection, Sam thought, and cursed under his breath as he crawled nearer.

The Sheriff did the same, aiming his weapon per his puppeteer. No doubt Perdifious could see the two advancing.

Again, Perdifious fired, this time from the side of the house. Seconds later, Sam heard glass crash, followed by an inner thud. Damn it, the bastard was inside.

Sam had to act fast, and he and his corpse lumbered to the front door. Sam grabbed the knob, but it did not budge, and so he had the Sheriff break the door down.

"Perdifious—where are you? Perdifious—hold your ground."

From upstairs, Perdifious growled, "You're in no position to demand anything, Cheveyo. You'll do as I say. Keep your rotted companion at bay, or I'll kill everyone up here, not only your flaccid friend, but the women. I'm not one to administer mercy. The child stands no better a chance."

Sam heard Cindy cry.

"I'm listening, Perdifious. What do you want?"

"You know what I want."

"What's the point? The Master will only make you his pawn after I hand the amulet over. Perhaps we should think this through, man to man, eye to eye."

"The Master is of no consequence to me. Perhaps I'll hoard the amulet to bargain for even more. I can do as I choose, you see, whereas you've no choice but to comply."

"Give me a moment." Sam thought it best to stall. "I need some time."

"You don't have that luxury. Give me the amulet or I'll go down the line. I'll make certain the child is first. All you need do is keep your corpse away and come to the door. I'll crack it open. You slip the object to me; an easy transaction. Every one satisfied. Every one alive."

Sam's mind tossed and turned. If only he could get into the room, but to do so, he needed a distraction.

Sam recalled the rear porch; small and roofed. Perhaps he and the Sheriff could enter from opposite ends; one from above, one from below. Sam could climb the porch post; make his way in from there. But was the plan feasible with so little time at hand?

Perdifious's fervor pulsated to the beat of his scars, influenced by the beckoning tension of O'Malley's mind. He called upon his demons to quell the essential but nagging thrust, but for whatever reason they did not reply.

At the foot of the bed, Cindy whimpered. Emily and Cassandra quivered to each side of it. O'Malley squirmed within his stupor.

Cassandra glanced at the folded cloth. Emily caught her eye and with a grimace urged her to make the move, but Cassandra could not muster the courage.

O'Malley moaned. Perdifious pointed his pistol at the man, but the flow of unconscious pulsations now growing annoying.

To the petrified women, Perdifious yapped, "Grab his pillow. Cover his face."

The women looked at each other, too frightened to budge.

Perdifious stomped. "Would you rather I ask the child?"

The women froze, even more stunned.

"Perhaps you'd rather I shoot him. It would prove a much quicker death." Perdifious heard footsteps. "Very well. For now, we'll let the inconsequential dullard be." He moved toward the door. "Who's there?" His tone was cautious yet sly. "I'll venture a guess. Could it be my red-skinned nemesis?"

Peridfious's tart inquiry prompted O'Malley to emit a long yowl, his ruffling consciousness smacking against Perdifious's brow. "Shut up, you damn fool."

The footsteps ceased.

Perdifious kept his gun on the women, his eyes on the door. "I trust you've removed the amulet." He pressed his lips against the wood. "Now, I'm going to open the door. Do you understand? I'm going to open, so that you may slip the amulet through."

"Yes," a soft, hoarse voice replied.

The overanxious Perdifious turned the knob, his eyes searching for a glint of the prize; his fingers extending into the dim hall, anxious to snatch it, but then the wafting decay filled his nose.

From behind, glass shattered. Sam had kicked through the window and tumbled onto the bedroom floor. Perdifious spun round, but Sam was swift enough to shoot the gun from his hand. On instinct, Perdifious rushed toward him and rammed Sam with all his vehement might.

Sam's lungs deflated. His focus faltered, leaving the Sheriff a hallway's stationary prop.

Perdifious then hammered upon Sam, knocking his gun loose, causing it to skid under the bed. Emily scooped Cindy into her arms, and Cassandra leapt toward the bureau. However, try as she may to grab the gun, she found Perdifious glancing her way, anchoring her hesitation. As Perdifious and Sam hobbled, struggled and stretched, Perdifious retrieved his weapon. Sam fell backward, landing on his rear, gasping.

Cassandra realized it was now or never, but just as she was finally about to spring, she noticed that O'Malley had cranked upward. His eyes widened past their unspectacled blur, landing upon the cloth. He nodded, and she nodded back.

Perdifious aimed his pistol at Sam, and with this, Cassandra snatched the concealed six-shooter and flung it straight into O'Malley's pale hand.

The gesture was enough to make Perdifious swivel, at which point O'Malley landed a bullet into his enemy's brow, hurling him against the wall.

Perdifious's eyes rolled upward in dazed disbelief, his scars darkening and curling, turning his complexion to a bright, vain violet.

"It can't be," he stammered. "It's...it's impossible....impossible."

But the impossible had become reality.

Perdifious's mind imploded, his spirit fighting its descent. He recalled the flames that consumed his childhood, the poisoned cake batter and Purity's fateful, Sunday morning. He thought of all the monstrous things he had done and had long wished to seize, how he had fostered them all with frigid patience, but now it all melted away, demon-less and infinite, nothing more than a lunatic's hollow dream.

Emily cupped Cindy's ears as O'Malley once more raised the six-shooter and fired with unparalleled precision, nailing Perdifious in the same spot, but this time reducing his head to globular mush.

At last, Sam caught his breath, the amulet burning against his skin. He forced himself up and stumbled forth as the Sheriff shambled in.

The women blinked in disbelief at the grisly display, at which time Cindy jiggled free from Emily and raced over to the Sheriff. She surprised them all by wrapping her arms around his rancid leg and to it muttered her thanks.

Sam calmed himself, as well as his puppet, not knowing what to say or do. He looked to the squinting O'Malley, who seemed more in awe of the scene.

Sam knelt, snatched his gun from under the bed and bounced up with a graceful glee. "Glad you woke up, Richard."

O'Malley mustered a laugh. "Same here." He tossed the six-shooter to the end of the bed. "I've had such strange visions, Sam. He coughed and winced. "I feel pretty weak, but I'm as pleased as punch to help." He looked at the child. "Say, there, little one. I appreciate your fondness for the Dead Sheriff, but aren't I the one to thank?"

Cindy turned and with a sweet whisper said, "I know, Mister O'Malley. I know. Pastor Wakefield told me you'd fix things. He saw it in his dreams. That's why I wanted to stay with you." She looked to Sam, then Emily, Cassandra and back up at the Sheriff. "He said the Dead Sheriff and Sam would make certain of it." She regarded Perdifious's shattered shell. "He promised me that you'd send the bad man to Hell."

O'Malley forced a grin, even if the child's words chilled him.

Sam then conducted few inconspicuous, finger moves, allowing the Sheriff to hoist Perdifious's frame like a rag doll over his shoulder and then accompanied the corpse at the threshold.

"Sorry for the mess, ladies." Sam gave a weary bow. "I'd help clean up, but I really should get back to the fighting."

"Fighting you say?" Emily stammered. "Oh, dear, what of our men?"

Cassandra suckled a sob. "Yes, are they still...alive?"

Sam only wished he could say. "When I last saw them, they were sure fighting the good fight. I've no doubt they're holding their own." He looked to O'Malley. "You're going to have a lot document, my friend, a lot to commemorate."

O'Malley fell backward, relishing and despising the prospect, as Cindy scooted to the puddle of blood that marked Perdifious's spot, enchanted if not comforted by the mountainous stain. So be it, thought Sam. Let her stare. She deserved the right to gloat.

He led the Dead Sheriff and Perdifious's husk from the room, leaving a long, incidental trail of blood as they headed through the house; just another rash reminder of the gruesome misfortunate that had befallen.

And yet the road before them would be all the better for Perdifious's demise, even if there was no telling what might yet wait ahead.

CHAPTER TWENTY-FOUR

They reached the heart of town in record time.

Sam heard shots ring out, but they were sporadic, leaving an uneasy, pervading silence.

Sam saw men slashed in half, others with perforated torsos, horses splattered and stomped, wagons cracked and splintered, their defunct occupants protruding with dulled, disbelieving eyes. Among them were women and children, not a lot perhaps, but enough to knot Sam's stomach.

Sam and the Dead Sheriff walked beyond the collapsed cannon, where Pendrake's lifeless body lay, gun in hand, head propped by a mangled daisy bed. Much the same went for Leigh a few feet yonder, sans a gun, his hands folded in strained prayer. No doubt the two had tried to survive, maybe even tried to defend themselves, as well as the town, but in the evident process, forfeited their lives. Neither wanted to fight, let alone die in this way. Sam respected their courage, though, but also blamed himself for it.

"Sam! Sam!" Kendle ran over, holding his rifle like a spear. "I've been looking for you." He regarded the Dead Sheriff and the dripping carcass he carted. "Good God, what happened?" He skipped to the rear of the living corpse and noted the headless man's attire. "It's him—Perdifious. How, Sam?"

"My friend, O'Malley broke from his stupor—shot the bastard twice to ensure he was dead."

"O'Malley? You mean to say you tracked Perdifious to Doc's home?"

Doc ran over, along with Elroy, their faces marred with dirt, dust and above all, woe.

"What was that you said, Paul? My home?" Doc looked at Sam and then the Dead Sheriiff. "Say, what's this? Who's he got there?"

"Their illustrious leader," Kendle confirmed. "Sam says he tracked him to your house. O'Malley killed him."

"O'Malley? Please, tell me, are the women all right?" He cringed, realizing that he had neglected to fill Kendle in. "I did leave Cassandra and the child with Emily. There was no time, Paul, none at all."

"They're fine, safe and sound," Sam assured them and then gestured at the fallen council members. "Wish I could say the same for those poor men." He looked about. "I imagine, there are more of Perdifous's men lurking about. Perhaps if they were to see his body—"

"No point," Elroy stated. "They're done—finished." He then glanced at the avenging corpse. "The Dead Sheriff shot 'em all, one after the other. He even picked up the guns of those he shot and used them against those that were yet comin'. It was a nonstop spree with six gun after six gun. Never seen anything like it. At one point, I swear—and yeah, it might have been all in my head, all a damn part of my imagination—but some of those men the Sheriff killed got up and shot those men still standing—the very men who were on their side. It was like he was using 'em as puppets. After it was all settled—and for the life of me, I thought it was going to go on forever—those rotten raiders were peppered across the ground. The Dead Sheriff just marched away, like he was being called to some other task or somethin', and now here he is with that depraved Perdifious hanging from his back."

"We combed the entire area, Sam," Kendle added, "to make certain that none of the gang remained. It's true. It's possible some fled, but my hunch is they're all dead. Sad thing is, among our own, the survival rate isn't great. Appears Judge Vincent got it, too; so did Sloan, the banker. We may have won the war, but we're in no position to brag." Kendle rubbed his eyes and smudged a few tears. "Was it worth it? Did we have any real choice? I keep telling myself what we did was necessary. I keep telling myself that if only we had been better prepared, had taken better measures to stop it in advance, more might be alive. Maybe..."

Sam was at a loss. His heart went out to Kendle. It was not the lawman's fault that pointless rage ran so rampant in the world. It always would, he suspected, whether guns, bayonets, cannons or gnashing teeth administered it. It did not validate the carnage, but the distasteful component remained an imbedded part of life and therefore, death: just part of what distinguished the pure from the impure, the good from the bad.

"We'll need to inform a higher authority of what's transpired," Doc remarked, his eyes bleary behind his skewed spectacles.

"I don't think there's any clear way to ascertain what's happened," Kendle explained, "no matter who inspects it. What's done is done, Doc. Ashes to ashes, don't you know?"

"What are we going to do with the bodies?" Elroy asked. "Not ours so much, but the others."

"The best you can do," Sam suggested, "is keep the two sides apart. Perdifious's remains, however, deserve special treatment."

Kendle found the comment odd. "How's that, Sam?"

"It seems our foe had a thing for fire. Let's just say I'd like to reciprocate."

Doc squinted. "Another Indian thing?"

Sam grinned. "Nope, Just a basic eye-for-an-eye thing."

Sam then guided the Dead Sheriff down the street. Their wagon appeared soon thereafter, its frightened horses chugging it along. Sam slowed them and directed the Dead Sheriff inside, where he dumped Perdifious's remains upon some blankets.

The Sheriff entered his casket, but before Sam threw down the canvas, he paused to say, "I don't know how it happened, if it was me or you or maybe the combination of us both, but I appreciate what you did. O'Malley's stunt was no doubt invaluable, but without you, we would've lost. I'm most certain of that." His eyes grew dewy, as he regarded the corpse. "Now, you have a long, deserved rest, my good man."

"Good man," the Dead Sheriff croaked, his milky orbs implying understanding.

Sam basked in the corpse's reassurance, draped the canvas over him and with renewed assurance, headed beyond Daisy Field.

He traveled as far as it felt right and then grabbed a match from O'Malley's belongings. He dragged Perdifious's husk across the grass and bracketed it with weeds and set them ablaze.

He watched the pyre with keen intent, curious if a hint of those guardian demons might manifest, but as the fire spread, he realized Perdifious's transcendental link no longer existed. Perhaps it never had, at least not as the villain believed.

The heat teased and tickled Sam, the amulet drawing the tantalizing warmth. No doubt the Master would be displeased and knowing that pleased Sam immeasurably.

Perdifious's spirit touched what felt like a flat, coarse surface, his soul throbbing as if it were one giant scar. The encompassing expanse was pitch-black night, he presumed, but where were the stars? Where and what was this place? Had his demons stashed him away into some bleak sanctuary to recoup?

He swung his indiscernible arms. "Where are you, demons? Show yourselves."

The silence was deafening.

"Come to me, damn it. Appear to me. I demand it."

From out the nothingness, a familiar voice reverberated: "You failed, Palmer Perdifious, but not as much as you have failed yourself."

Perdifious reeled at the Master's dissatisfied tone.

"Please, I'll try again. I can still seize the amulet. I assure you. I—I implore you."

"I have no time for vain promises. There is nothing more you can offer me. I am only here to punctuate your fate."

Perdifious bubbled with rage. "You don't intimidate me, Master. I am Hades's sacred son—protected by a horde far stronger than you, far stronger than anything in this universe."

The Master laughed. "Stronger, you say? Are you serious? I must say, your view of Hell is weak. Your pact was never made with it. Search as you will, you will never gain what you thought you had, for it never existed in the way you had hoped." The Master's tone softened, as if to imply sorrow for the wretched soul. "You are your own devil, Palmer Perdifious, your own creation. From the time you were a child, you carved that mad, dubious distinction."

Perdifious's soul quivered. Was the pact he had forged so long ago no more than a misdirected whim?

"I was wrong about you, Palmer Perdifious. I cannot respect evil if it is not aligned with forces that are true. From nothingness you forged your fate, your fairy demons and now into nothingness, you shall forever circle."

"No, please." Perdifious felt the darkness thicken. "Please, no."

He reached up, imagining that his earthly flesh was within reach. If only he could re-enter his body, reactivate his organs, regrow his goddamn head. Then a chilling revelation gripped him. His body was no more. It had been devoured by flame, reduced to ashes.

The beginning of the end had come for Palmer Perdifious. His great, callous heights no longer mattered. His alleged, carved-in-stone fate had been deposited upon a fickle, open-ended road.

Palmer Perdifious would remain scarred within his own virulent ruminations, wandering among his allegorical weeds, no more than a pathetic spark dancing along an open stretch of intangible flames. Palmer Perdifious had become one with his own inverted prophesy, a one-and-only Lucifer in a one-and-only Hell, and along with that dubious distinction, he experienced more fear, more despair than when he was an infant.

Emily tucked Cindy in, pecked her cheek and shut the door.

The child could hear her guardians' whispers.

"We might as well continue tending to her."

"It wouldn't be right otherwise, Paul."

"And it is the least we can do."

"Of course. She's been through so much."

Cindy felt their warmth. It was comforting and yet it seemed to stem well beyond their tones, manifesting right within her room.

She sat up and blinked at the burgeoning, bright light and focused on the familiar figure that formed from out it.

Cindy smiled. "Hello, Pastor."

The immaculate specter, dressed as he would on any Sunday morn, placed his finger to his lips.

She nodded and lowered her voice. "It went just as you said. Mister O'Malley did it. They all helped. The bad man's dead."

Wakefield nodded. "And the same goes for the others who harmed us. It's all over now, Cindy. You can put it behind you."

Her eyes teared. "But I don't think I can, Pastor. I can't forget it. I keep trying, but it still hurts."

The pastor considered the matter and sighed. "Then you've no choice but to look ahead. That's all you can do, my dear. In fact, it's all that any of us can do in the wake of tragedy."

Wakefield then dissolved, breaking apart like a dying star, only to pave the way for other, shimmering shapes.

Cindy's eyes grew wide and when she recognized the manifestations, she trembled with joy.

"It's all right, Cindy," her father said, looking smooth and dignified, the light streaming from the seams of his Sunday best. "Pastor Wakefield is correct. What's done is done. The past can't be changed."

"If anything," cooed her mother, looking more radiant than Cindy could have ever recalled, "it will make you stronger when the days turn dark."

"And dark days are part of any life. They sneak up on you, Cindy, hit when you least expect them."

"Like that day at the church?" Cindy said.

"Yes," her father validated.

"But wrongs can be made right," her mother stated.

"And goodness can triumph if one believes." Her father's eyes gleamed. "Besides, you're stronger, tougher now. You'll carry on just fine, and you have good people to help you. They'll look after you."

"If you open your heart to them," her mother cooed, "they'll give you all the happiness you deserve. You'll gain all that we wished to give you and so much more and even more, give unto others."

Her parents then faded away just as Wakefield had.

Cindy felt a great weight lifted from her, from the entire town, in fact. Spirits moved from out the air and into a place where peace and forgiveness reigned supreme. Indeed, Paradise welcomed those marred by despair. It opened its gates to orphans who had died before their time, to churchgoers who perished on a Sunday morn that had first promised such joy, to men who fought hard even though doctrine begged them to turn the cheek. It was a place for the meek and misguided, for the cheated and soured, for all those who had lost their way, but wished to regain it more than anything that life or death could bring.

Someday she would join them, embrace them one and all, but for now, she had her life to live. For now, she would only nurture good thoughts, embrace the good fortune she had been bestowed: what God and His angels had given her. They would look after her; ensure that she would become a person they would be honored to call their own.

It was her unswerving, carved-in-stone fate. The winged, haloed entities that circled her bed told her so, and that was enough to fortify her unflinching faith.

EPILOGUE

One Month Later

Doc checked O'Malley's eyes. "You look fine, but I wouldn't push it much, and keep those dang cigars at a minimum. You don't want a relapse."

O'Malley climbed onto the wagon and took his place alongside Sam. "I promise, Doc, I'll be careful, and if not, Sam here will set me straight. If he doesn't, well, there's a congenial chap waiting in the back who'll be glad to do it."

Doc chuckled. "And what about you, Sam? What's on the agenda?"

"Purposeful adventure, Doc, and if good fortune should shine, a few dollars more to sweeten the pot."

"Amen to that," O'Malley chimed.

Kendle approached, along with Emily and Cindy, the child tugging her surrogate parents' fingers as she swayed between them. Elroy followed, watching the display with complacency.

"Why, hello," O'Malley addressed the quartet with a tip of his new, short brimmed hat. "So glad you came to see us off."

"We wouldn't have it any other way," Kendle confirmed. "It's sure gonna be odd without you fellows around. Elroy, for one, is taking it real hard."

Elroy shrugged. "Seems safer with you here, is all. Besides, got the cannon fixed. Wanted to show it off, but don't want those government gents to confiscate it."

"Keep it covered," Sam advised. "It hasn't been easy for us, either. A canvassed box, in particular a putrid one, can draw attention."

Marshals and rangers milled about, more to chat than deduce. They had combed Purity's charred remnants and noted traces of Daisy Field's bloodshed. Slivers of a carcass off the beaten path had also been found: the likely, barbaric work of "natives" who saw fit to exit their territories, the officials deduced. Whatever the case or conclusion, it was now all a matter of formal documentation, though O'Malley was far better equipped to handle the historic account than any of them, with enough details at his disposal to span inexhaustible editions.

Sam regarded Kendle, Cindy and Emily, their semblances serene. He appreciated their gratitude, as they did his.

"I wish you the best of luck," Sam told Doc. "Give my regards to Cassie."

"Same here," said O'Malley. "She proved an exemplary nurse. I am forever in her debt, as I am yours."

Sam pointed to Elroy. "And that goes for you, too, Mister Elroy—without question, one of the bravest, most resourceful men I've ever had the pleasure to meet."

Doc and Elroy smiled, but their postures implied a fatigue that would not subside anytime soon. At least they could take pride in having paid their dues. In Sam's estimation, that was worth more than a thousand compliments.

With goodbyes sealed, Sam struck the group an amiable salute and prompted the wagon forward, but as it rolled, Kendle reached inside and gave the casket a solid pat.

"Remember, Cheveyo—keep strikin' fear into those bad men."

Sam glanced back at the stalwart lawman, his smiling spouse and placid lass. "For the sake of the good ones, Paul, consider it done."

From there they passed a set of graveyards: to the left, the interred marauders, their spots wracked by thick, withering weeds and to the right, those who had lost their lives to sustain a way of life, their beds adorned with heartfelt care, around which prolific patches of daises reached toward a sky clear, blue and pure.

FROM THE JOURNAL OF RICHARD O'MALLEY:

"For the sake of the good ones..." Never have words rung so true, and they will distinguish my writings from henceforth, ensuring that vile men live on edge, no matter where they roam.

To impress this, the Dead Sheriff's legend grows greater each day. Some believe in him, some do not, but the division between good and evil will be better defined because of the debate, leaving the most profound impression on those who frown upon brutality, corruption and impunity; all those bitter things that decent folks wish the world would shed.

But do not fret. As long as the Dead Sheriff lives, justice can—and will—prevail. On that you have my solemn pledge, Cheveyo's and of course, the Dead Sheriff's.

THE END

ABOUT OUR CREATORS

WRITER -

MICHAEL HOUSEL - Over the years, has penned horror, science-fiction and psychodrama short stories, as well as reviews for toy and hobbyist periodicals. He is also the author of the monster-rally novel, "Flask of Eyes", published by Caliburn Press. You may visit his blog at http://bizarrechats. blogspot.com, where he offers reflections on a variety of fantasy-based topics.

INTERIOR ILLUSTRATOR -

ROB DAVIS - began his professional art career doing illustrations for role-playing games in the late 1980's. Soon after he began lettering and inking, then penciling comics for a number of small black and white comics publishers. Most notably for Eternity Comics—which eventually became Malibu Comics in the 1990's—on their book SCIMIDAR with writer R.A. Jones. Branching out to other black and white publishers and eventually working at both DC and Marvel Rob worked on likeness intensive comics like comic book adaptations of television shows QUANTUM LEAP and STAR TREK's many incarnations though primarily DEEP SPACE NINE comics for Malibu. At Marvel he worked on the Saturday morning cartoon adaptation PIRATES OF DARK WATER. After the comics industry implosion in the late 1990's Rob picked up work on video games, advertising illustration and T-shirt design as well as some small press comics like ROBYN OF SHERWOOD for Caliber and TWILIGHT GRIMM for Silverline. Rob continues to do the odd self-published comic book as well as publisher and designer for his small-press production REDBUD STUDIO COMICS. Rob is Art Director, Designer and Illustrator for the New Pulp production outfit AIRSHIP 27 partnered with writer/editor Ron Fortier. Rob is the recipient of the PULP FACTORY AWARD for "Best Interior Illustrations" in 2010 and 2016 for his work on SHERLOCK HOLMES: CONSULTING DETECTIVE and has been nominated for the same award numerous times. Now fully retired from "real work" he lives in central Missouri with his wife and two children.

COVER ARTIST -

MICHAEL YOUNGBLOOD – Of Asheville N.C. has a bachelor's degree in art and has done most of his work in architectural illustration and design. He's also done various other freelance projects since 1991.

Richard O'Malley is a hard working Boston reporter in the years following the Civil War. He is fascinated by tales of the wild west and the colorful frontiersmen who are taming it. None captivate him more than the stories of the Dead Sheriff; a dedicated lawman who had risen from the grave to continue his mission. Taking his life savings, O'Malley embarks on a personal quest to find this mythical figure and chronicle his exploits. What he finds will make them both legends.

Airship 27 Productions is thrilled to bring pulp fans Mark Justice's most original creation in this new, expanded edition; the first of a brand new series starring...

PULP FICTION FOR A NEW GENERATION!